Francis Hopkinson Smith

A Day at Laguerre's and Other Days

Being nine sketches

Francis Hopkinson Smith

A Day at Laguerre's and Other Days
Being nine sketches

ISBN/EAN: 9783337097097

Printed in Europe, USA, Canada, Australia, Japan

Cover: Foto ©Andreas Hilbeck / pixelio.de

More available books at **www.hansebooks.com**

A DAY AT LAGUERRE'S
AND OTHER DAYS

A DAY AT LAGUERRE'S AND OTHER DAYS BEING NINE SKETCHES BY F. HOPKINSON SMITH

BOSTON AND NEW YORK HOUGHTON MIFFLIN AND COMPANY THE RIVERSIDE PRESS CAMBRIDGE MDCCCXCII

TO MY OUT-DOOR FRIENDS
EVERYWHERE: MY GOOD
ESPERO, WHOM I LOVE;
MANUEL AND HIS SWEET-
HEART; LITTLE LUCETTE
WITH THE VELVET EYES; BIG-
HEARTED CAPTAIN JOE, AND EVEN
ISAACS—
ISAAC ISAACS,
THE UNFAITHFUL, WHO IS WATCH-
ING TO FLEECE ME AGAIN WHEN
NEXT I VISIT CONSTANTINOPLE

THE INTRODUCTION TO THE READER

HESE slight sketches are the records of some more idle days, stolen, I must confess, from a busy and far more practical life. I have committed these depredations upon myself for years, and have then run off to the far corners of the earth and sat down in some forgotten nook to enjoy my plunder.

The villainy, strange to say, has only served to open my eyes the wider — and my heart too for that matter — and to bring me closer to many fellow tramps who have delighted my soul, and still do.

Idle tramps if you will, who love the sunlight and simple fare and simple ways; ne'er-do-wells, who haunt the cafés and breakfast at twelve; vagrants made millionaires by a melon and a cigarette; mendicants who own a donkey and a pair of panniers, have three feast days a week, earn but half a handful of copper coin, and sing all day for the very joy of living.

If you too can unhook your neck from the new car of Juggernaut— American Progress—which is crushing out the sweetness of an old-timed, simpler life, and would gain a little freedom, turn bandit yourself. If you have the pluck to take a long rest, the sun is still blazing along the Grand Canal in dear old Venice. If you can only muster up courage for a short breathing spell, — even a day, — there is still a chop to be served under the vines overhanging the Bronx.

The stories are all true. Many of the names are genuine, and everybody is still alive. Most of them will be waiting for me when I run off again.

F. H. S.

New York, March, 1892.

A TABLE OF THE CONTENTS OF THIS BOOK

I. A DAY AT LAGUERRE'S

T is the most delightful of French inns, in the quaintest of French settlements. As you rush by in one of the innumerable trains that pass it daily, you may catch glimpses of tall trees trailing their branches in the still stream, — hardly a dozen yards wide, — of flocks of white ducks paddling together, and of queer punts drawn up on the shelving shore or tied to soggy, patched-up landing-stairs.

If the sun shines, you can see, now and then, between the trees, a figure kneeling at the water's edge, bending over a pile of clothes, washing, — her head bound with a red handkerchief.

If you are quick, the miniature river will open just before you round the curve, disclosing in the distance groups of willows, and a rickety foot-bridge perched up on poles to keep it dry. All this you see in a flash.

But you must stop at the old-fashioned station, within ten minutes of the
Harlem River, cross the road, skirt
an old garden bound with a fence and
bursting with flowers, and so pass on
through a bare field to the water's edge,
before you catch sight of the cosy little
houses lining the banks, with garden
fences cutting into the water, the arbors covered with tangled vines, and the
boats crossing back and forth.

I have a love for the out-of-the-way
places of the earth when they bristle all
over with the quaint and the old and
the odd, and are mouldy with the picturesque. But here is an in-the-way place,
all sunshine and shimmer, with never a
fringe of mould upon it, and yet you lose
your heart at a glance. It is as charming in its boat life as an old Holland
canal; it is as delightful in its shore life
as the Seine; and it is as picturesque
and entrancing in its sylvan beauty as
the most exquisite of English streams.

The thousands of workaday souls who
pass this spot daily in their whirl out
and in the great city may catch all these
glimpses of shade and sunlight over the
edges of their journals, and any one of
them living near the city's centre, with
a stout pair of legs in his knickerbockers
and the breath of the morning in his

heart, can reach it afoot any day before breakfast; and yet not one in a hundred knows that this ideal nook exists.

Even this small percentage would be apt to tell of the delights of Devonshire and of the charm of the upper Thames, with its tall rushes and low-thatched houses and quaint bridges, as if the picturesque ended there; forgetting that right here at home there wanders many a stream with its breast all silver that the trees courtesy to as it sings through meadows waist-high in lush grass, — as exquisite a picture as can be found this beautiful land over.

So, this being an old tramping-ground of mine, I have left the station with its noise and dust behind me this lovely morning in June, have stopped long enough to twist a bunch of sweet peas through the garden fence, and am standing on the bank waiting for some sign of life at Madame Laguerre's. I discover that there is no boat on my side of the stream. But that is of no moment. On the other side, within a biscuit's toss, so narrow is it, there are two boats; and on the landing-wharf, which is only a few planks wide, supporting a tumbledown flight of steps leading to a vine-covered terrace above, rest the oars.

3

I lay my traps down on the bank and begin at the top of my voice : —

"Madame Laguerre! Madame Laguerre! Send Lucette with the boat."

For a long time there is no response. A young girl drawing water a short distance below, hearing my cries, says she will come; and some children above, who know me, begin paddling over. I decline them all. Experience tells me it is better to wait for madame.

In a few minutes she pushes aside the leaves, peers through, and calls out: —

"Ah! it is that horrible painter. Go away! I have nothing for you. You are hungry again that you come?"

"Very, madame. Where is Lucette?"

"Lucette! Lucette! It is always Lucette. Luc-e-t-t-e!" This in a shrill key. "It is the painter. Come quick."

I have known Lucette for years, even when she was a barefooted little tanglehair, peeping at me with her great brown eyes from beneath her ragged straw hat. She wears highheeled slippers now, and sometimes on Sundays dainty silk stockings, and her hair is braided down her back, little French Marguérite that she is, and her hat is never ragged any more, nor her hair tangled. Her eyes, though, are still the same velvety, half-drooping

4

eyes, always opening and shutting and never still.

As she springs into the boat and pulls towards me I note how round and trim she is, and before we have landed at Madame Laguerre's feet I have counted up Lucette's birthdays, — those that I know myself, — and find to my surprise that she must be eighteen. We have always been the best of friends, Lucette and I, ever since she looked over my shoulder years ago and watched me dot in the outlines of her boat, with her dog Mustif sitting demurely in the bow.

Madame, her mother, begins again:—

"Do you know that it is Saturday that you come again to bother? Now it will be a *filet*, of course, with mushrooms and tomato salad; and there are no mushrooms, and no tomatoes, and nothing. You are horrible. Then, when I get it ready, you say you will come at three. 'Yes, madame; at three,' — mimicking me, — 'sure, very sure.' But it is four, five, o'clock — and then everything is burned up waiting. Ah! I know you."

This goes on always, and has for years. Presently she softens, for she is the most tender-hearted of women, and would do anything in the world to please me.

5

" But, then, you will be tired, and of
course you must have something. I remember now there is a chicken. How
will the chicken do ? Oh, the chicken
it is lovely, *charmant*. And some pease
— fresh. Monsieur picked them himself
this morning. And some Roquefort,
with an olive. Ah ! You leave it to
me ; but at three — no later — not one
minute. *Sacré ! Vous êtes le diable!*"

As we walk under the arbor and by
the great trees, towards the cottage,
Lucette following with the oars, I in-
quire after monsieur, and find that he is
in the city, and very well and very busy,
and will return at sundown. He has a
shop of his own in the upper part where
he makes *passe-partouts*. Here, at his
home, madame maintains a simple restaurant for tramps like me.

These delightful people are old friends
of mine, François Laguerre and his wife
and their only child Lucette. They
have lived here for nearly a quarter of a
century. He is a straight, silver-haired
old Frenchman of sixty, who left Paris,
between two suns, nearly forty years
ago, with a gendarme close at his heels,
a red cockade under his coat, and an
intense hatred in his heart for that " little nobody," Napoleon III.

If you met him on the boulevard you

6

would look for the decoration on his lapel, remarking to yourself, " Some retired officer on half pay." If you met him at the railway station opposite you would say, " A French professor returning to his school." Both of these surmises are partly wrong, and both partly right. Monsieur Laguerre has had a history. One can see by the deep lines in his forehead and by the firm set of his eyes and mouth that it has been an eventful one.

His wife is a few years his junior, short and stout, and thoroughly French down to the very toes of her felt slippers. She is devoted to François and Lucette, the best of cooks, and, in spite of her scoldings, good - nature itself. As soon as she hears me calling there arise before her the visions of many delightful dinners prepared for me by her own hand and ready to the minute — all spoiled by my belated sketches. So she begins to scold before I am out of the boat or in it, for that matter.

Across the fence next to Laguerre's lives a *confrère*, a brother exile, Monsieur Marmosette, who also has a shop in the city, where he carves fine ivories. Monsieur Marmosette has only one son. He too is named François, after his father's old friend. Farther down on both sides

7

of the narrow stream front the cottages
of other friends, all Frenchmen; and
near the propped-up bridge an Italian
who knew Garibaldi burrows in a low,
slanting cabin, which is covered with
vines. I remember a dish of *spaghetti*
under those vines, and a flask of Chianti
from its cellar, all cobwebs and plaited
straw, that left a taste of Venice in my
mouth for days.

As there is only the great bridge
above, which helps the country road
across the little stream, and the little
foot-bridge below, and as there is no
path or road, — all the houses fronting
the water, — the Bronx here is really
the only highway, and so everybody must
needs keep a boat. This is why the
stream is crowded in the warm after-
noons with all sorts of water crafts
loaded with whole families, even to the
babies, taking the air, or crossing from
bank to bank in their daily pursuits.

There is a quality which one never
sees in nature until she has been rough-
handled by man and has outlived the
usage. It is the picturesque. In the
deep recesses of the primeval forest,
along the mountain-slope, and away up
the tumbling brook, nature may be majestic, beautiful, and even sublime ; but
she is never picturesque. This quality

comes only after the axe and the saw have let the sunlight into the dense tangle and have scattered the falling timber, or the round of the water-wheel has divided the rush of the brook. It is so here. Some hundred years ago, along this quiet, silvery stream were encamped the troops of the struggling colonies, and, later, the great estates of the survivors stretched on each side for miles. The willows that now fringe these banks were saplings then ; and they and the great butternuts were only spared because their arching limbs shaded the cattle knee - deep along the shelving banks.

Then came the long interval that succeeds that deadly conversion of the once sweet farming lands, redolent with clover, into that barren waste — suburban property. The conflict that had lasted since the days when the pioneer's axe first rang through the stillness of the forest was nearly over ; nature saw her chance, took courage, and began that regeneration which is exclusively her own. The weeds ran riot ; tall grasses shot up into the sunlight, concealing the once well-trimmed banks ; and great tangles of underbrush and alders made lusty efforts to hide the traces of man's unceasing cruelty. Lastly came this lit-

9

tle group of poor people from the Seine and the Marne and lent a helping hand, bringing with them something of their old life at home, — their boats, rude landings, patched-up water-stairs, fences, arbors, and vine-covered cottages, — unconsciously completing the picture and adding the one thing needful — a human touch. So nature, having outlived the wrongs of a hundred years, has here with busy fingers so woven a web of weed, moss, trailing vine, and low-branching tree that there is seen a newer and more entrancing quality in her beauty, which, for want of a better term, we call the picturesque.

But madame is calling that the big boat must be bailed out ; that if I am ever coming back to dinner it is absolutely necessary that I should go away. This boat is not of extraordinary size. It is called the big boat from the fact that it has one more seat than the one in which Lucette rowed me over ; and not being much in use except on Sunday, is generally half full of water. Lucette insists on doing the bailing. She has very often performed this service, and I have always considered it as included in the curious scrawl of a bill which madame gravely presents at the end of each of my days here, beginning

in small printed type with " François
Laguerre, Restaurant Français," and
ending with " Coffee 10 cents."

But this time I resist, remarking that
she will hurt her hands and soil her
shoes, and that it is all right as it is.

To this François the younger, who is
leaning over the fence, agrees, telling
Lucette to wait until he gets a pail.

Lucette catches his eye, colors a little,
and says she will fetch it.

There is a break in the palings through
which they both disappear, but I am half-
way out on the stream, with my traps
and umbrella on the seat in front and
my coat and waistcoat tucked under the
bow, before they return.

For half a mile down-stream there is
barely a current. Then comes a break
of a dozen yards just below the perched-
up bridge, and the stream divides, one
part rushing like a mill-race, and the
other spreading itself softly around the
roots of leaning willows, oozing through
beds of water-plants, and creeping under
masses of wild grapes and underbrush.
Below this is a broad pasture fringed
with another and larger growth of willows. Here the weeds are breast-high,
and in early autumn they burst into purple asters, and white immortelles, and
goldenrod, and flaming sumac.

11

If a painter had a lifetime to spare, and loved this sort of material, — the willows, hillsides, and winding stream, — he would grow old and weary before he could paint it all ; and yet no two of his compositions need be alike. I have tied my boat under these same willows for ten years back, and I have not yet exhausted one corner of this neglected pasture.

There may be those who go a-fishing and enjoy it. The arranging and selecting of flies, the joining of rods, the prospective comfort in high water-boots, the creel with the leather strap, — every crease in it a reminder of some day without care or fret, — all this may bring the flush to the cheek and the eager kindling of the eye, and a certain sort of rest and happiness may come with it; but — they have never gone a-sketching ! Hauled up on the wet bank in the long grass is your boat, with the frayed end of the painter tied around some willow that offers a helping root. Within a stone's throw, under a great branching of gnarled trees, is a nook where the curious sun, peeping at you through the interlaced leaves, will stencil Japanese shadows on your white umbrella. Then the trap is unstrapped, the stool opened, the easel put up, and you set your pa-

12

lette. The critical eye with which you look over your brush-case and the care with which you try each feather point upon your thumb-nail are but an index of your enjoyment.

Now you are ready. You loosen your cravat, hang your coat to some rustic peg in the creviced bark of the tree behind you, seize a bit of charcoal from your bag, sweep your eye around, and dash in a few guiding strokes. Above is a turquoise sky filled with soft white clouds ; behind you the great trunks of the many-branched willows ; and away off, under the hot sun, the yellow-green of the wasted pasture, dotted with patches of rock and weeds, and hemmed in by the low hills that slope to the curving stream.

It is high noon. There is a stillness in the air that impresses you, broken only by the low murmur of the brook behind and the ceaseless song of the grasshopper among the weeds in front. A tired bumblebee hums past, rolls lazily over a clover blossom at your feet, and has his midday luncheon. Under the maples near the river's bend stands a group of horses, their heads touching. In the brook below are the patient cattle, with patches of sunlight gilding and bronzing their backs and

13

sides. Every now and then a breath of
cool air starts out from some shaded
retreat, plays around your forehead, and
passes on. All nature rests. It is her
noontime.

But you work on : an enthusiasm has
taken possession o you ; the paints mix
too slowly ; you use your thumb, smear-
ing and blending with a bit of rag —
anything for the effect. One moment
you are glued to your seat, your eye
riveted on your canvas, the next, you
are up and backing away, taking it in
as a whole, then pouncing down upon it
quickly, belaboring it with your brush.
Soon the trees take shape ; the sky
forms become definite ; the meadow lies
flat and loses itself in the fringe of willows.

When all of this begins to grow upon
your once blank canvas, and some lucky
pat matches the exact tone of blue-gray
haze or shimmer of leaf, or some ac-
cidental blending of color delights you
with its truth, a tingling goes down your
backbone, and a rush surges through
your veins that stirs you as nothing else
in your whole life will ever do. The re-
action comes the next day when, in the
cold light of your studio, you see how
far short you have come and how crude
and false is your Lest touch compared

14

with the glory of the landscape in your mind and heart. But the thrill that it gave you will linger forever.

But I hear a voice behind me calling out : —

"Monsieur, mamma says that dinner will be ready in half an hour. Please do not be late."

It is Lucette. She and François have come down in the other boat — the one with the little seat. They have moved so noiselessly that I have not even heard them. The sketch is nearly finished ; and so, remembering the good madame, and the Roquefort, and the olives, and the many times I have kept her waiting, I wash my brushes at once, throw my traps into the boat, and pull back through the winding turn, François taking the mill-race, and in the swiftest part springing to the bank and towing Lucette, who sits in the stern, her white skirts tucked around her dainty feet.

"*Sacré!* He is here. *C'est merveilleux!* Why did you come ? "

"Because you sent for me, madame, and I am hungry."

"*Mon Dieu!* He is hungry, and no chicken ! "

It is true. The chicken was served that morning to another tramp for breakfast, and madame had forgotten all about

15

it, and had ransacked the settlement for its mate. She was too honest a cook to chase another into the frying-pan.

But there was a *filet* with mushrooms, and a most surprising salad of chicory fresh from the garden, and the pease were certain, and the Roquefort and the olives beyond question. All this she tells me as I walk past the table covered with a snow-white cloth and spread under the grape-vines overlooking the stream, with the trees standing against the sky, their long shadows wrinkling down into the water.

I enter the summer kitchen built out into the garden, which also covers the old well, let down the bucket, and then, taking the clean crash towel from its hook, place the basin on the bench in the sunlight, and plunge my head into the cool water. Madame regards me curiously, her arms akimbo, re-hangs the towel, and asks : —

"Well, what about the wine ? The same ? "

"Yes ; but I will get it myself."

The cellar is underneath the larger house. Outside is an old-fashioned, sloping double door. These doors are always open, and a cool smell of damp straw flavored with vinegar from a leaky keg greets you as you descend into its

16

recesses. On the hard earthen floor rest *A Day at*
eight or ten great casks. The walls are *Laguerre's*
lined with bottles large and small, loaded on shelves to which little white cards
are tacked giving the vintage and brand.
In one corner, under the small window,
you will find dozens of boxes of French
delicacies — truffles, pease, mushrooms,
pâté de foie gras, mustard, and the like,
and behind them rows of olive oil and
olives. I carefully draw out a bottle
from the row on the last shelf nearest
the corner, mount the steps, and place
it on the table. Madame examines the
cork, and puts down the bottle, remarking sententiously : —
"Château Lamonte, '62 ! Monsieur
has told you."
There may be ways of dining more
delicious than out in the open air under
the vines in the cool of the afternoon,
with Lucette, in her whitest of aprons,
flitting about, and madame garnishing
the dishes each in turn, and there may
be better bottles of honest red wine to
be found up and down this world of care
than "Château Lamonte, '62," but I
have not yet discovered them.
Lucette serves the coffee in a little
cup, and leaves the Roquefort and the
cigarettes on the table just as the sun
is sinking behind the hill skirting the

17

railroad. While I am blowing rings
through the grape leaves over my head
a quick noise is heard across the stream.
Lucette runs past me through the garden, picking up her oars as she goes.

" *Oui, mon père.* I am coming."

It is monsieur from his day's work in
the city.

"Who is here?" I hear him say as
he mounts the terrace steps. " Oh, the
painter — good!"

" Ah, *mon ami.* So you must see the
willows once more. Have you not tired
of them yet?" Then, seating himself,
" I hope madame has taken good care of
you. What, the '62? Ah, I remember
I told you."

When it is quite dark he joins me under the leaves, bringing a second bottle
a little better corked he thinks, and the
talk drifts into his early life.

"What year was that, monsieur?"
I asked.

" In 1849. I was a young fellow just
grown. I had learned my trade in
Rheims, and I had come down to Paris
to make my bread. Two years later
came the little affair of December 2.
That ' nobody,' Louis, had dissolved the
National Assembly and the Council of
State, and had issued his address to the
army. Paris was in a ferment. By the

18

help of his soldiers and police he had A Day at Laguerre's
silenced every voice in Paris except his
own. He had suppressed all the journals, and locked up everybody who had
opposed him. Victor Hugo was in exile,
Louis Blanc in London, Changarnier
and Cavaignac in prison. At the moment I was working in a little shop near
the Porte St. Martin decorating lacquer-
work. We workmen all belonged to a
secret society which met nightly in a
back room over a wine-shop near the
Rue Royale. We had but one thought
— how to upset the little devil at the
Élysée. Among my comrades was a big
fellow from my own city, one Cambier.
He was the leader. On the ground
floor of the shop was built a huge oven
where the lacquer was baked. At night
this was made hot with charcoal and
allowed to cool off in the morning ready
for the finished work of the previous day.
It was Cambier's duty to attend to this
oven.

"One night just after all but he and
two others had left the shop a strange
man was discovered in a closet where the
men kept their working clothes. He
was seized, brought to the light, and instantly recognized as a member of the
secret police.

"At daylight the next morning I was

19

aroused from my bed, and, looking up, saw Chapot, an inspector of police, standing over me. He had known me from a boy, and was a friend of my father's.

"'François, there is trouble at the shop. A police agent has been murdered. His body was found in the oven. Cambier is under arrest. I know what you have been doing, but I also know that in this you have had no hand. Here are one hundred francs. Leave Paris in an hour.'

"I put the money in my pocket, tied my clothes in a bundle, and that night was on my way to Havre, and the next week set sail for here."

"And what became of Cambier?" I asked.

"I have never heard from that day to this, so I think they must have snuffed him out."

Then he drifted into his early life here — the weary tramping of the streets day after day, the half - starving result, the language and people unknown. Suddenly, somewhere in the lower part of the city, he espied a card tacked outside of a window bearing this inscription, "Decorator wanted." A man inside was painting one of the old-fashioned iron tea-trays common in those days. Monsieur took off his hat, pointed to the card, then to himself, seized the brush, and before the man could protest had covered the bottom with morning-glories so pink and fresh that his troubles ended on the spot. The first week he earned six dollars; but then this was to be paid at the end of it. For these six days he subsisted on one meal a day. This he ate at a restaurant where at night he washed dishes and blacked the head waiter's boots. When Saturday came, and the money was counted out in his hand, he thrust it into his pocket, left the shop, and sat down on a doorstep outside to think.

" And, *mon ami*, what did I do first?"

" Got something to eat?"

" Never. I paid for a bath, had my hair cut and my face shaved, bought a shirt and collar, and then went back to the restaurant where I had washed dishes the night before, and the head waiter *served me*. After that it was easy; the next week it was ten dollars; then in a few years I had a place of my own; then came madame and Lucette—and here we are."

The twilight had faded into a velvet blue, sprinkled with stars. The lantern which madame had hung against the arbor shed a yellow light, throwing into clear relief the sharply cut features of

21

monsieur. Up and down the silent
stream drifted here and there a phan-
tom boat, the gleam of its light following
like a firefly. From some came no sound
but the muffled plash of the oars. From
others floated stray bits of song and
laughter. Far up the stream I heard
the distant whistle of the down train.

"It is mine, monsieur. Will you cross
with me, and bring back the boat?"

Monsieur unhooked the lantern, and
I followed through the garden and down
the terrace steps.

At the water's edge was a bench holding two figures.

Monsieur turned his lantern, and the
light fell upon the face of young François.

When the bow grated on the opposite
bank I shook his hand, and said, in parting, pointing to the lovers, —

"The same old story, monsieur?"

"Yes; and always new. You must
come to the church."

II. ESPERO GORGONI, GON-DOLIER

OOR old Ingenio — my gondolier of five years before — dear old Ingenio, with his white hair and gentle voice ; Ingenio with the little, crippled daughter and the sad-faced wife, who lived near the church behind the Rialto, had made his last crossing. At least the sacristan shook his head and pointed upward when I sought tidings of him ; and the old, familiar door with the queer gratings was locked, and the windows cobwebbed and dust-begrimed.

None of the gondoliers at the Rialto landing knew, nor did any of the old men at the water-steps — the men with the hooked staffs who steady your boat while you alight. Five years was so very long ago, they said, and then there had been the plague.

So I looked up wistfully at the windows of the old palace where I had called to him so often — I can see him now, with little Giuliétta in his arms, peering at me through the gay, climbing flowers which she watered so care-fully — looked long and wistfully, as if he must surely answer back, " *Si, signore, immediatamente,*" and turned sadly away.

But then there was the same old gon-dola-landing, blue poles, bridge, and all, with its flock of gondolas hovering around, and a dozen lusty fellows ready to spring to their oars and serve me night and day for a pittance that else-where a man would starve on. My lucky star once sent me Ingenio, who floating past caught my signal ; why not another?

This is why I am on the quay near the Rialto this lovely morning, in Ven-ice, overlooking the gondolas curving in and out, and watching the faces of the gondoliers as with uplifted hands, like a row of whips, they call out their respec-tive numbers and qualifications.

In my experience there is nothing like a gondola to paint from, especially in the summer — and it is the summer time. Then all these Venetian cabs are gay in their sunshiny attire, and have laid aside their dark, hooded cloaks, their rainy - day mackintoshes — their *felsi* — and have pulled over their shoul-ders a frail awning of creamy white, with snowy draperies at sides and back, under which you paint in state or lounge

24

luxuriously, drinking in the beauty about you.

I have in my wanderings tried all sorts of moving studios : *tartanas* in Spain, *volantes* in Cuba, broad-sailed luggers in Holland, mules in Mexico, and cabs everywhere. One I remember with delight — an old night-hawk in Amsterdam — that offered me not only its front seat for my easel, its arm-rest for my water-bottle, and a pocket in the door flap for brushes (I am likely to expect all these conveniences in even the most disreputable of cabs), but insisted on giving me the additional luxury of a knot-hole in its floor for waste water.

But with all this a cab is not a gondola.

In a gondola you are never shaken by the tired beast resting his other leg, nor by the small boy who looks in at the window, nor by the cabby, who falls asleep on the box and awakes periodically with a start that repeats a shiver through your brush hand, and a corresponding wave-line across your sky.

In place of this there is only a cosy curtain-closed nest — a little boudoir with down cushions and silk fringes and soft morocco coverings; kept afloat by a long, lithe, swan-like, moving boat, black as an Inquisitor's gown save for

25

the dainty awning. A something bearing itself proudly with head high in air,
—alive or still, alert or restful, and
obedient to your lightest touch,—half
sea-gull reveling in the sunlight, half
dolphin cutting the dark water.

If you are hurried, and the plash of
the oar comes quick and strong, in an
instant your gondola quivers with the
excitement of the chase. You feel the
thrill through its entire length as it
strains every nerve; the touch of the
oar, like the touch of the spur, urging
it to its best. If you would rest, and
so slip into some dark waterway under
the shadow of overhanging balcony or
mouldy palace wall, your water-swallow
becomes a very *lasagnone*, and will go
sound asleep, and for hours, or loll lazily, the little waves lapping about its
bow.

In Venice my gondola is always my
home, and my gondolier always my best
friend; and so when my search for Ingenio ended only in a cobwebbed door
and an abandoned balcony, and that
mournful shake of the sacristan's head,
and I stood scanning anxiously the upturned faces below me, it was some minutes before I selected his successor and
returned Espero's signal.

I cannot say why I singled him out

except, perhaps, that he did not press *Espero Gorgoni, Gondolier* forward with the rest, rushing his bow ahead; but rather held back, giving his place to a gray-headed old gondolier, who in his haste had muffed his oar awkwardly, at which the others laughed.

Perhaps, too, it might have been his frank, handsome, young face, with its merry, black eyes; or the inviting look of the cushions beneath the white awning, with the bit of a rug on the floor; or the picturesque effect of the whole; or all of them together, that caught my eye. Or it might have been the perfect welding together of man and boat. For, as he stood erect in the sunlight, twisting the gondola with his oar, his loose shirt, with throat and chest bare in highest light against the dark water, his head bound with a red kerchief, his well-knit, graceful figure swaying in the movement of the whole, — blending with and yet controlling it, — both man and boat seemed but parts of one organism, a sort of marine Centaur, as free and fearless as that wonderful myth of the olden time. Whatever it was, my lucky star peeped out at the opportune moment, and the next instant my sketch-traps were tumbled in.

"To the Salute!"

The gondolier threw himself on his

27

oar, the sensitive craft quivered at the touch, and we glided out upon the broad waters of the Grand Canal.

Nowhere else in the wide world is there such a sight. A double row of creamy white palaces tiled in red and topped with quaint chimneys. Over-hanging balconies of marble, fringed with flowers, with gay awnings above and streaming shadows below. Two lines of narrow quays crowded with people flash-ing bright bits of color in the blazing sun. Swarms of gondolas, barcos, and lesser water-spiders darting in and out. Lazy red - sailed luggers, melon - loaded, with crinkled green shadows crawling be-neath their bows ; while at the far end over the glistening highway, beaded with people, curves the beautiful bridge — an ivory arch against a turquoise sky.

Espero ran the gauntlet of the skim-ming boats, dodging the little steamers puffing away all out of breath with their run from the Lido, shot his boat into a narrow canal, and out again upon the broad water, until the edge of her steel blade touched the water-stairs of the Sa-lute.

This beautiful church is always my rendezvous. It is half-way to every-thing : to the Public Garden ; across the Giudecca ; away over to the Lagoon

where the fishermen live ; to the Rialto
and beyond.

In the freshness of the morning, when its lovely dome throws a cool shadow across its piazza, there is no better place for a painter to make up his mind as to where he would work. Mine required but a few minutes ; I would paint near the Fondimenta della Pallada ; a narrow, short canal where the fishermen moor their boats.

"What is your name, gondolier ? "

"Espero Gorgoni."

The voice was sweet and musical, and the answer was given with a turn of the head as graceful as it was free.

"Do you know the Pallada ? "

"Perfectly."

"Stop, then, where the crab baskets are moored to the poles."

A turn of the wrist, a long, bending sweep of the oar across the Giudecca, and we enter a waterway leading to the Lagoon. Here live the fishermen, in great, rambling houses three and four stories high, — warehouses probably in the old days, — running sheer into the water. Outside of the lower windows lie their boats, with gay-colored sails, and next to these stand a row of poles anchoring the huge wicker crab and fish baskets filled with their early morning catch.

29

Espero ran the gondola behind a protecting sail, and in five minutes I was at
work.

The experience was not new to him.
I saw that from the way he opened the
awning on the proper side, unstrapped
my easel, and spread out the contents of
my trap on the cushions, which he reversed to protect from waste water ; and
from the way he stepped ashore, so that
my gondola should lie perfectly still,
joining later a group of children who
were watching me from the doorway
above. (Half an hour after they were
laughing at his stories, the two young-
est in his lap.) A considerate, good-natured fellow, I thought, — this gondolier
of mine, — and fond of children ; and I
kept at work.

When the fisherman awoke and came
down to make ready his boat for the
morning, and I began the customary
protest about the lowering of the sail,
thus spoiling my sketch, Espero sprang
up, locked his arm through that of the
intruder, and led him gently back into
the house, calling to me, five minutes
thereafter, from across the canal, to keep
at work and not to hurry, as the fisherman and he would have a mouthful of
wine together. And a man of tact,
too ! Really, if my gondolier develops

30

like this, I shall not miss Ingenio so
much.

The next day we were across the Lagoon, and the day following up the Giudecca, by the storehouses where the lighters unload, and before the week was out I had fallen into my old habits and was sharing my breakfast and my cigarette-case with my gondolier, who, day by day, won his way by some new trait of usefulness or some new charm of manner.

Oh, these breakfasts in the gondola in the early morning; the soft, fresh air of the sea in your face, the cool plash of the water in your ears! On the floor of the boat, smoking hot, rests the little copper coffee-pot; above in the wooden side-pockets, your store of fruit and rolls. With what a waste and recklessness is the melon split and quartered, and the half-eaten crescents thrown overboard! What savory fish! What delicious bread! What luscious figs! And yet Espero had gathered them all up at a caffè, a fruit-stand, and a baker's; and a bit of silver no larger than my thumbnail had paid for it all.

When the wind freshens and the boats from Chioggia begin spreading their sails, Espero turns his prow toward the

31

Public Garden, — their mooring-ground, — and we follow them out over the broad water until my sketch-book is filled with their varying forms and colors. On our way back we board the wood boats, drifting in with the tide, or land under the old garden - walls, which Espero scales, regaining the gondola loaded with flowers, which he festoons over the awning, trailing the blossoming vines in the water behind. Or we circle about the Salute, composing it now on the right, with some lighter boats in the distance ; now on the left, with the Dogana and the stretch of palaces beyond. Or we haunt the churches, listening to the music, or follow with our eyes the slender, graceful Venetians who come and go.

In all these rambles there was one little, crooked canal near the Salute that, whatever our course, Espero always dodged into. Long way around or short way over, it was always the same. Somehow Espero must get into this waterway to get out somewhere else. At last I caught him. She wore a yellow silk handkerchief tied under her pretty chin and was waving her hand from a balcony filled with oleanders high up on the wall of a crumbling old palace. These were our days !

Then came the twilights, with palace, tower, and dome purple in the fading light, the canal all molten gold, the gondolas, with lamps alight, gliding like fireflies.

On one of these purple-laden twilights we had floated over to San Giorgio, moored the gondola to a great iron ring in the water-soaked steps that might once have held a slave-laden galley, and had sat down to watch the darkness as it slowly settled over the dreaming city. Away off to the right stood the Campanile, its cone-shaped top pink and gold, while behind, against the deepening blue, rose its twin tower.

The scene awoke all the old memories, and I began talking to Espero, who was stretched out on the marble steps below me, of the olden times when this same harbor was full of ships of every clime, with sails of gold and cargoes of spice, and of the great regattas, and the two-decked war barges, with slaves double-banked rowing beneath ; and from this to the wonderful Bucentaur, the Doge's barge, encrusted with gold, rowed by the members of the Arsenalotti — a sort of guild or corporation formed of the workmen at the Arsenal. How, every year, occurred the ceremony of the Espousal of the Adriatic, and how, when the Bu-

33

centaur returned, there was a grand banquet, at which the Arsenalotti dined at the public expense, with the privilege of carrying off everything on the table — even the linen, vessels, and glass.

Espero's attitude and face, as he listened, led me on. He had an odd way of lifting his eyebrows quickly when I told him something that interested him, — a questioning, yet deferential expression, which I generally accepted as a tribute to my superior intelligence. He never formulated it in words. It was only one of the many flashes that swept over his face, but it was always a grateful encouragement.

And so, with the glamour of the scene about me, and with Espero's eyes fastened on mine, his well-shaped head clear cut against the fading sky, I rambled on, telling him of those things I thought would please him the most. Of how these Arsenalotti became gondoliers, joining the Castellani, — the gondoliers at that time being divided into two parties, the Castellani, who wore red hoods, and the Nicolletti, who wore black hoods. Of how these Castellani were aristocrats and had portioned out to them the eastern part of the city where the Doge lived, his residence being in the Piazza of San Marco ; while the Nicolletti were

34

only publicans. That, besides attending to the Doge in public, many of these Castellani had served him in private, thus being of great service to the state.

Espero listened to every word, raising his head and looking at me curiously when I mentioned the Castellani, and laughing outright at my description of the banquet tables in the hands of the Arsenalotti. Nothing else dropped from his lips except the grim remark that if he had lived in those days he would, perhaps, have owned his own gondola, and not have had to use his grandfather's, who was now too old to row. I remembered afterward that a certain thoughtful expression overspread his face, as if my talk had awakened some memory of his own.

A passing music boat cut short my dissertation, and in a moment more we were following in its wake, threading our way in and out of the tangle of gondolas massed about it. Then a twist of the oar, and Espero glided alongside the lantern-hung barge and leaned over to speak to the leader. The musicians were going to the Piazza, would I care to hear them sing under the Bridge of Sighs?

In five minutes we had picked our way through the labyrinth of surround-

35

ing gondolas, and in five more had entered the close, narrow canal, where the beautiful bridge, buttressed by two great masses of gloom, — the palace and the prison, — overhung the sluggish, sullen water.

There is never a lantern now along this weird and grewsome waterway. One only sees the twinkling lamps of the gondolas, like will-o'-the-wisps, drift past, — the boats themselves lost in the blackness of the shadows, — the glimmer of the pale light of some slow-moving barge, or the reflection of the stars above. All else is dark and ghostly.

The music boat drifted sideways, and the bass viol, who was standing, twisted a light cord through an iron ring in the slimy, ooze-colored palace. Espero drifted against the opposite wall — the prison.

"What shall they sing, signor?"

"As you please, Espero."

I have heard the Miserere chanted at dead of night in the streets of an old Italian town, the flare of the torches lighting the upturned face of the ghastly dead; my eyes have filled when, with knee to marble floor, I have listened to the pathos of its harmonies sighing through the many-pillared mosque of Cordova; I have drunk in its cadences

36

in curtained alcoves with the breath of waving fans and flash of gems about me; but never has its grandeur and majesty so stirred my imagination and entranced my soul as on this night in Venice, under the deep blue of the soft Italian sky, the frowning, blood-stained palace above, the treacherous silent water beneath.

I could stretch out my hand and touch the very stones that had coffined the living dead. I could look down into the same depths along the edge of the water-soaked marble where had lain the headless body, with sack and cord, awaiting the sure current of the changing tide; and from my cushions in the listening gondola I could see, high up against the blue in the starlight, the same narrow window in the fatal arch, through which the hopeless had caught a last glimpse of light and life.

When the last low strains had died away, Espero raised himself erect, walked slowly the length of the gondola, and, bending down, said in a voice tremulous with emotion, "Signor, did you hear the tramp of the poor fellows over the bridge, and the moans of the men dying under the wall? Holy God! Was it not terrible?"

At that instant the barge floated past.

37

I looked at him in wonder — Espero's eyes were full of tears!

This man began to interest me intensely. Only an every-day, plain, Venetian gondolier, in a blue shirt, and patched at that, with hardly a franc he could call his own, and yet there was something about him that made his presence a delight. It was not the graceful swing of his beautiful body, nor his musical laugh, nor his honest kindness to every human being. It was rather an undefined, courteous, well - bred independence.

When it came to rowing a gondola, it never seemed to me that he rowed because it was his duty and his livelihood. He rowed because he loved it, and because he loved the sunshine across his face and the flash of the water on his oar-blade — the swing and freedom of it all. My happening to be a passenger was but one of those necessary evils attending the earning and payment of five francs a day. And yet, not altogether an evil; for he loved me, too, as he did everything else that brought him companionship and air and light and life.

Nothing seemed to tire him. Day or

38

night, or all night, if I wished it — for *Espero*
often we were whole nights together in *Gorgoni,*
the soft summer air, floating back to *Gondolier*
the sleeping city in the gray dawn, stopping to listen to early mass at the Pieta,
or following the fruit boats or fishermen
in from the Lido.

And thus it was that we ransacked
Venice from San Giorgio to Murano;
and thus it was that every day I caught
some fresh glimpse of the sweetness of
his inner nature, and every day loved
him the better. Nobody could have
helped it. There was that touch about
him one could not resist. Once on the
Giudecca, when the sea was polished
steel and the tide turning ebb, Espero
ran the gondola up under the lee of a
melon boat, its sail limp and useless in
the breathless air, sprang over her rail,
caught the oar from the captain, fagged
out with the long pull from the Lido,
and threw his weight against the drooping blade. And all this with a laugh
and a twist of his foot in pirouette, as if
it was the merriest fun in the world to
save a tide and a market for a man he
had never seen in his life before.

On another morning he was just in
time to save Beppo from a plunge overboard — old Beppo who for centuries
(nobody knows how old Beppo is) has

hooked his staff into myriads of gondolas landing at the Salute steps. It had happened that some other mediæval ruin, a few years Beppo's junior, had crowded the old man from his place, and Espero's righteous wrath was not appeased until he had driven the usurper from the piazza of the church, with the parting reminder that he would break every bone in his withered old skin if he ever caught him there again.

And yet, with all my opportunities for intimacy, I really got no nearer to the inner side of Espero than the day I hired him. To him I was still only the painter from over the sea, his patron, to whom he was loyal, good-natured, happy-hearted, and obliging; but nothing more. Nothing more was for sale for five francs a day. What his home or life might be outside the hours I called my own, I knew no more than of the hundred other gondoliers who filled the canal with their cries and their laughter. The one sole connecting link was the pretty Venetian of the little, crooked canal, who waved her hand whenever we passed, and who once tossed down a spray of oleander which fell at his feet; and yet I could not even have found her doorway, much less have told her name.

One beautiful, bright Sunday morn- ing, perplexed at this unequal exchange of confidences, this idea took possession of me. Espèro and I would breakfast together — blue shirt, patch, and all! Not as we had often breakfasted before, in the gondola under the shadow of a palace, or down by the stalls of the fruit market; but at the great Caffè Florian, in the Piazza of San Marco, at twelve o'clock, high noon, in the midst of gold embroidered officers with clanking swords and waxed mustaches, and ladies of high degree in dainty gowns and veils.

"Leave the gondola, Espero, in charge of somebody, and come with me!"

We twisted our way through the narrow slits of streets, choked with awnings shading groups of Venetians sipping their coffee, dodged under an archway, across a narrow bridge, and so out upon the blinding, baking Piazza, dotted here and there with hurrying figures, dogged by ink-spilled shadows.

"Breakfast for two!" I said to the startled waiter. "Take the seat by the window, Espero!"

His face lighted up, and an expression of the greatest happiness and good-humor overspread it. But that was all. There was no sign of humility; nothing indicating that I had done him a kind-

41

ness, or had conferred upon him any special favor. He merely pointed to himself, and then to the seat, as if making quite sure, saying, " Me, signor ? " and then sat himself down, spreading his napkin, and all with the air of a man accustomed to that sort of thing every day of his life.

I ordered nearly everything on the bill of fare. Fish, eggs, salad, broiled cutlet, fruit, even a bottle of Chianti, with silk tassels on its neck. Espero took each in its course with the easy grace of a Chesterfield, and the quiet refinement of a man of the world.

The only person who put his astonishment into words was the head waiter, who caught his breath when I lighted Espero's cigarette myself, recounting to his assistant, and adding, " *Ma foi*, what funny people these painters ! "

An hour later we were again afloat, embarking at the water-steps of the Piazza.

Just here, and for the first time in all our intercourse, I noticed a change in Espero's bearing. The touch of humility — it had been only a trace, and, as I always knew, only assumed that I might see he recognized the obligation of five francs — even that slight touch was gone.

The change was not one that beto-

42

kened presuming familiarity, as if all so-
cial barriers having now been swept
away he would insist upon sharing with
me everything I owned. It was more
the manner of a man clothed with the
responsibilities of a host; a welcoming,
generous, appropriating manner. Here-
tofore, when I had stepped into the gondola, Espero invariably offered me his
bent elbow to steady myself; but now
he gave me his hand.

Furthermore, he did not wait for in-
structions as to where the prow of the
gondola should be pointed. He said,
instead : —

" There is a famous old Cortile that I
must show you. All the artists paint it.
We will go now ! "

With this he shot past our customary
landing-place, entered the little, crooked
canal, and rounded the gondola in front
of an old marble archway curiously
carved.

I began to wonder at the change that
had come over him. What was there
about this Cortile ? If everybody had
painted it, why should he have kept it
hidden all summer from me ?

Espero's manner at this landing was,
if anything, more expressive than at the
last ; for, after securing the gondola, he
waved his hand graciously and led me

along a damp, tunnel-like passage, until we stepped into an abandoned cloister, once the most beautiful Cortile in Venice.

When we entered the sun was blazing against the opposite wall, the nearer columns standing out strong and dark. In the square, bounded by the low wall supporting the pillars, which in turn supported the living rooms above, climbing vines and grasses ran riot, while in the centre of the tangled mass of weeds stood an old covered well, at which a girl was filling her copper water-pail.

Espero watched my delight at its picturesqueness, laughing outright at my determination to begin work at once, and then, with great deference, led me to a doorway level with the flagging of the mouldy pavement. Here he rang a bell hung on the outside. The next instant a shutter opened above and a pair of black eyes peered out from between some pots of oleanders. It was the same face I had seen so often smiling at Espero from an upper balcony! The cloister evidently abutted on the little, crooked canal. This, then, was what he was hiding! But surely he could not have thought that I would have stolen his sweetheart!

Another moment and the door was

44

opened by the same pretty Venetian, who ushered us into a square hall having a broad staircase which led to the floor above. Here, on the wainscoted walls, half way to the ceiling, hung a collection of old portraits, each one a delight to the eye of a painter. They were of men, costumed in the time of the later Doges — one in scarlet and black, another in a robe of deep blue, while a third wore a semi-military uniform and carried a short sword.

They all had one distinguishing feature : each head was covered by a bright red hood.

Espero never took his eyes from my face as I looked about me in astonishment, not even long enough to salute the pretty Venetian who stood smiling at his side.

" Who lives here, Espero ? "

" My grandfather, signor, who is very old, lives on this floor. My little wife, Mariana," turning to the pretty Venetian, "and I live on the floor above ; " and he kissed the girl on the forehead and laid her hand in mine.

" And these portraits " —

" Are some of the famous gondoliers of old. This one was chief of the Arsenalotti, and an intimate friend of the Doge."

45

"And the others?"

Espero's eyes twinkled, and a quizzical, half-triumphant smile broke over his face.

"These are all my ancestors, signor. We have been gondoliers for two hundred years. I am a Castellani!"

III. UNDER THE MINARETS

IT was a small, not over-clean, and much-crumpled card.

It was held very near my nose, and above the heads of a struggling, snarling pack of Turks, Armenians, Greeks, and Jews, all yelling at the tops of their voices, and all held at bay by a protecting rail in the station and two befezzed officers attached to the custom-house of his Serene Highness. It bore this inscription : —

Isaac Isaacs,

Dragoman and Interpreter,

Constantinople.

Beyond this seething mass of Orientals was seen an open door, and through this only the sunlight, a patch of green grass, and the glimpse of a minaret against the blue.

Yes ; one thing more — the card.

The owner carried it aloft, like a flag of truce. He had escaped the tax-gathering section of the Sublime Porte by dodging under the guarded rail, and with fez to earth was now pressing its oblong proportions within an inch of my eyeglasses.

"Do you speak English?"

"Ev'ting: Yerman, Franche, Grek, Tearkish — all!"

"Take this sketch-trap, and get me a carriage."

The fez righted itself, and I looked into the face of a swarthy, dark-bearded mongrel, with a tobacco-colored complexion and a watery eye. He was gasping for breath and reeking with perspiration, the back of his hand serving as sponge.

I handed him my check, — through baggage Orient Express, two days from Vienna, — stepped into the half-parched garden, and drank in my first full breath of Eastern air.

Within the garden — an oasis, barely kept alive by periodical sprinkling — lounged a few railroad officials hugging scant shadows, and one lone Turk dispensing cooling drinks beneath a huge umbrella.

Outside the garden's protecting fence wandered half the lost tribes of the earth. Some staggered under huge

casks of wine swung on poles; some
bent under cases as large as pianos;
some were hawking bread, Turkish
sweets, grapes, and sugared figs; some
were peddling clothes, some sandals,
some water-jars: each splitting the air
with a combination of shouts and cries
that would have done justice to a traveling menagerie two hours late for breakfast. In and out this motley mob
slouched the dogs — in the middle of the
street, under the benches, in everybody's
way and under everybody's feet : everywhere dogs, dogs, dogs!

Beyond this babel straggled a low
building attached to the station. Above
rose a ragged hill crowned by a shim-
mering wall of dazzling white, topped
with rounded dome and slender minarets.
Over all was the beautiful sky of the
East, the joy and despair of every brush
from the earliest times down to my own.

Ever since the days of the Arabian
Nights — my days — the days of Ha-
roun al Raschid, of the big jars with the
forty scalded thieves and the beautiful
Fatima with the almond-shaped eyes, I
have dreamed of the Orient and its
palaces of marble. And so, when Baron

49

de Hirsch had brought the home of the Caliphs within two days' journey of the domes of San Marco, I threw some extra canvases into a trunk, tucked a passport into my inside pocket, shouldered my sketch-trap, and bought a second-class ticket for Constantinople.

I had only one object — to paint.

My comrades at Florian's — that most delightful of caffès on the Piazza — when they heard that I was about to exchange the cool canals of my beloved Venice for the dusty highways of the unspeakable Turk, condemned my departure as quixotic. The fleas would devour me; the beggars (all bandits) steal my last franc; and the government lock me up the very first moment I loosened my sketch-trap.

But Isaac Isaacs, the dragoman, is standing obsequiously with fez in hand, two little rivulets of well-earned sweat coursing down each cheek.

"Ze baggages ees complet, effendi."

Isaac crawled upon the box, the driver, a barelegged Turk with fez and stomach sash, drove his heel into the haunches of the near horse, once, no doubt, the pride of the desert, and we whirled away in a cloud of dust.

"I don't see my trunk, Isaac."

"Not presently, effendi. It now arrives immediatamente at the dogane. Trust me!"

Five minutes more, and we alighted at the custom-house.

"This way, effendi."

For the benefit of those unfamiliar with the liquid language of the Orient, I will say that effendi means master, and that it is never applied except to some distinguished person — one who has, or is expected to have, the sum of half a piastre about his person.

Isaac presented the check — a scrap of paper — to another befezzed official, and the next moment ushered me into a small room on the ground-floor, furnished with a divan, a tray with coffee and cigarettes, and an overfed, cross-legged Turk. There was also a secretary, curled up somewhere in a corner, scratching away with a pen.

I salaamed to the Turk, detailed into the secretary's ear an account of my birth and ancestry, my several occupations and ambitions, my early life at home, my past life in Venice, and my present intentions in Constantinople. I then opened my passport, sketch-book, and trap, and delivered up the key of my trunk.

The secretary undid his legs, stamped upon my official passport a monogram of authority looking more like the image of a fish-worm petrified in the last agonies of death than any written sign with which I was familiar, and clapped his hands in a perfectly natural Aladdin sort of way. A genie in the shape of a Nubian, immeasurably black, moved from behind a curtain, and in five minutes my trunk holding the extra canvases, with a great white cross of peace chalked upon its face, was strapped to the carriage, and we on our way to the Royal.

As I said before, I had come to Constantinople to paint. Not to study its exquisite palaces and mosques ; its marvelous stuffs ; its romantic history ; its religion, the most profound and impressive ; its commerce, industries, and customs ; but simply to paint. To revel in color ; to sit for hours following with reverent pencil the details of an architecture unrivaled on the globe ; to watch the sun scale the hills of Scutari, and shatter its lances against the fairy minarets of Stamboul ; to catch the swing and plash of the rowers rounding their caïques by the bridge of Galata ; to wander through bazaar, plaza, and market, dotting down splashes of robe, turban, and sash ; to rest for hours in cool tiled mosques, with the silence of the

52

infinite about me; to steep my soul in a Under the Minarets
splendor which in its very decay is sub-
lime; and to study a people whose rags
are symphonies of color, whose traditions and records the sweetest poems of
modern times.   If you are content with
only this, then come with me to the patio of the Mosque Bayazid — the Pigeon
Mosque.

Isaac Isaacs, dragoman, stands at its
door, with one hand over his heart, the
other raised aloft, invoking the condem-
nation of the gods if he lies.   In his
earnestness he is pushing back his fez,
disclosing an ugly old scar in his wrin-
kled, leathery forehead — a sabre cut, he
tells me, in a burst of confidence, won
in the last row with Russia.   His black
beard is shaking like a goat's, while his
hands, with upturned palms and thumbs,
touch his shoulders with the old wavy
motion common to his race.   Standing
now in the shadow of the archway, he
insists that no unbeliever is ever per-
mitted to make pictures in the patio,
where flows the sacred fountain, and
where the priests and faithful wash
their feet before entering the holy temple.

I had heard something like this before.
The idlers at Florian's had all said so;
an intelligent Greek merchant whom I

53

met on the train had been sure of it;
and even the clerk of the Royal shrugged
his shoulders and thought I had better
not.

All this time — Isaac still invoking
new gods — I was gazing into the most
beautiful patio along the Golden Horn,
feasting my eyes on columns of verd-
antique supporting arches light as rain-
bows.

Crossing the threshold, I dropped my
trap behind a protecting column, and
ran my eye around the Moorish square.
The sun blazed down on glistening mar-
bles; gnarled old cedars twisted themselves upward against the sky; flocks
of pigeons whirled and swooped and fell
in showers on cornice, roof, and dome;
and tall minarets, like shafts of light,
shot up into the blue. Scattered over
the uneven pavement, patched with
strips and squares of shadows, lounged
groups of priests in bewildering robes
of mauve, corn-yellow, white and sea-
green, while back beneath the cool arches
bunches of natives listlessly pursued
their several avocations.

It was a sight that brought the blood
with a rush to my cheek. Here at last
was the East, the land of my dreams!
That swarthy Mussulman at his little
square table mending seals; that fellow

next him selling herbs, sprawled out on the marble floor, too lazy to crawl away from the slant of the sunshine slipping through the ragged awning; and that young Turk in frayed and soiled embroidered jacket, holding up strings of beads to the priests passing in and out, — had I not seen them over and over again?

And the old public scribe with the gray beard and white turban writing letters, the motionless veiled figures squatting around him, was he not Baba Mustapha, and the soft-eyed girl whispering into his ear none other than Morgiana, " fair as the meridian sun "?

Was I to devour all this with my eyes, and fill my soul with its beauty, and take nothing away? My mind was made up the moment I looked into the old scribe's face. Once get the confidence of this secret repository of half the love-making and intrigue in Stamboul, and I was safe.

" Isaac ! "

" Yes, effendi."

" Do you know the scribe ? "

Isaac advanced a step, scrutinized the old patriarch for a moment, and replied, —

" Effendi, pardonnez, he the one only man in Stamboul I not know."

This time, I noticed, he omitted the invocation to the gods.

"Then I'll present you."

I waited until the scribe looked up and caught my eye. Then I bowed my head reverently, and gave him the Turkish salute. It is a most respectful salutation. You stoop to the ground, pick up an imaginary handful of dust, press it to your heart, lips, and forehead in token of your sincerity and esteem, and then scatter it to the four winds of heaven. Rapidly done, it looks like brushing off a fly.

The old scribe arose with the dignity of King Solomon — I am quite sure he looked like him — and offered me his own straw-thatched stool. I accepted it gravely, and opened my cigarette case.

He unseated a client, dismissed his business for the day, and sat down beside me. Then, Isaac interpreting, I turned my sketch-book leaf by leaf, ·showing him bits of Venice, and in the back of the book some tall minarets of an old mosque caught on my way through Bulgaria.

It was curious to watch his face as the dragoman located for him the several scraps and blots, and explained their meaning. He evidently had never seen their like before. When he came to the

56

minaret, his eye brightened, and point- *Under the*
ing upward to the one above our heads, *Minarets*
he drew an imaginary outline with his
hand, and pointed to me. I nodded my
head. At this he looked grave, and I .
forthwith sent Isaac for coffee, and
lighted another cigarette. Before the
cups were emptied I had formally and
with great ceremony asked and received
permission to paint the most sacred
patio, Isaac protesting all the time in
high dudgeon as he unbuckled my trap,
that the scribe was a common pauper,
earning but a spoonful of copper coin
in a day, with no more right to grant
me a permit than the flea-bitten beggar at the gate. It was evident that
Isaac had not come to Constantinople
to paint.

Half an hour later, the arches were
sketched in, the pillars and roof line
complete, and I rapidly nearing that
part in my work in which the pencil is
exchanged for my palette, when the
shrill voice of the muezzin calling the
faithful to prayer sounded above my
head. I could see his little white dot
of a turban bobbing away high above
me on the minaret, his blue robe waving in the soft air.

In an instant priests, seal-maker, herb-
doctor, and peddler crowded about the

57

fountain, washed their faces and feet, and moved silently and reverently into the mosque. Soon the patio was deserted by all except Isaac, the pigeons, and the scribe, — the kindly old scribe, — who remained glued to his seat, lost in wonder.

Another hour, and the worshipers came straggling back, resuming their several avocations. Last of all came the priests, in groups of eight or ten, flashing masses of color as they stepped out of the cool arches into the blinding sunlight. They approached my easel with that easy rhythmic movement, so gracefully accentuated by their flowing robes, stopped short, and silently grouped themselves about me. I had now the creamy white of the minaret sharp against the blue, and the entrance of the mosque in clear relief.

For an instant there was a hurried consultation. Then a beardless young priest courteously but firmly expounded to Isaac some of the fundamental doctrines of the Mohammedan faith, — this one in particular, "Thou shalt not paint."

Before I could call to Isaac, I felt a hand caress my shoulder, and raised my head. The scribe, with faded robe gathered about him, stood gazing into the

58

face of the speaker. I held my breath, Under the
wondering whether, after all, I had left Minarets
San Marco in vain. Isaac remained
mute, a half-triumphant " I told you so "
expression lighting up his face.

Then the old scribe waved Isaac
aside, and, drawing himself to his full
height, his long beard blending with his
white robe, answered in his stead. " I
have given my word to the Frank. He
is not a giaour, but a true Moslem, a
holy man, who loves our temple. I have
broken bread with him. He is my friend,
bone of my bone, blood of my blood.
You cannot drive him away."

After that, painting about Constantinople became quite easy. Perhaps the
priests told it to their fellow-priests,
who spread it abroad among the faithful in the mosques; perhaps the gossips
around the patio took it up, or the good
scribe whispered it into the veiled ear
of his next fair client, and so gave it
wings. How it happened, I know not;
but from that day my white umbrella
became a banner of peace, and my open
sketch-book a passport to everybody's
courtesy and everybody's good will.

59

Let me remind those who may have forgotten it that there is really no such place as Constantinople. There is, of course, the old Turkish city of Stamboul, with all the great mosques: the mosque of the Six Minarets; the Sultana Valedé; Soliman, and some hundred others — and where, moreover, one finds the great bazaar — twelve miles of arcaded streets in a tangle — the caffès, drug-markets, fish-markets, spice-markets, vile-smelling, dirt-choked alleys and baths.

Then there is the European city of Pera, up a hill, — a long way up, — with its modern tramway below, and the ancient tower of the Genoise crowning the top. Pera, rebuilt since the fire, with its new hotels and foreign embassies, its modern shops filled with machine-made Oriental embroideries, and its more modern streets flanked by the everlasting four-story house with the flat roof and balcony, and the same old cast-iron railings and half-dead potted plants. Pera, the commonplace, except, perhaps, for one delightfully picturesque old cemetery with its curious headstones and dismal cypresses which could not be burned, and so could not be rebuilt and ruined.

And last, across the Bosphorus, is Scutari, only ten minutes by ferry-boat. Scutari-in-Asia, with mosques, archways, palaces, seraglios, fruit-markets, Arab horses, priests, eunuchs with bevies of houris out for an airing, gay awnings, silks in festoons from shop doors, streets crowded with carnival-like people wearing every color under the sun, Bedouins on horseback riding rapidly through narrow streets, tons and tons of grapes piled up in baskets, soldiers in fez and brown linen suits:—everything that is foreign and un-European, and out of the common world. A bewildering, overwhelming, intoxicating sight to a man who has traveled one half the world over to find the picturesque, and who suddenly comes upon all there is in the other half crammed into one compact mass a mile square.

Isaac never quite understands why I go about absorbed in these things, and why I ignore the regulation sights—the mosque with the Persian tiles, three miles away and a carriage; the treasury at Seraglio Point, opened only by permit from the Grand Vizier (price £2); the dancing dervishes at Pera; the howling dervishes at Scutari; and the

61

identical spot where Leander plunged into the sea.

I finally compromised with Isaac on the dervishes. We had spent the morning at Scutari, where I had been painting an old mosque. It was howling-dervish day, — it comes but once a week, the howl beginning at three P. M. precisely, — and to satisfy Isaac I had left the sunshine for an hour to watch their curious service.

I had, it is proper to state, wrung a confession that morning from Isaac which had so humiliated him that he had suggested the dervishes to divert my attention. A dragoman of the opposition, a veritable son of Abraham, had betrayed him. He had bitten his thumb at him, not literally but figuratively, and this in very decent English — no, the reverse. He had charged him with fraud. He had said that his name was not Isaac Isaacs, but Yapouly — Dreco Yapouly; that he was not an honest Jew, but a dog of a Turk, who had stolen honest Isaac's name when he died. Yes, robbed him, ghoul, grave-digger, beast! He with a scar on his forehead, where he had been branded for theft! And here the opposition dragoman snatched Isaac's fez from his head, and ground it into the dirt with his heel.

After a gendarme had taken this very disagreeable opposition dragoman away, Isaac had confessed. So many Englishmen, Frenchmen, Americans, he said, had wanted Mr. Isaacs that he had concluded that it was cruel not to accommodate them. Of what use, estimable effendi, was a dead Jew? How infinitely better a live Turk! So one day, when hanging over the rail at the station, an Englishman had arrived holding the deceased Isaac's card in his hand, and since that time Yapouly had been Isaac Isaacs to the stranger and the wayfaring man. " See, effendi, here the Angleeshman card."

It was the same the rascal had pressed into my own face!

Thus it was that Dreco Yapouly Isaacs — I will no longer lend myself to his villainous deception — preceded me this day up a steep hill paved with boulders, entered the low door of the *tekkè* (house) of the dervishes, and motioned me to a seat in a small open court sheltered by an arbor covered with vines.

In the centre was a well flagged by a great stone, and on this rested a high narrow-necked silver pitcher of perfect Oriental shape used by the priests in their ablutions. At the door of the sacred room stood a stalwart Nubian

63

dressed in pure white — ten times as black by contrast.

Five francs, and we passed the hanging curtain covering the entrance, and stepped inside a square, low-ceiled room hung with tambourines, cymbals, arms, and banners, and surrounded on three sides by an aisle.

The howlers — there were at least a dozen — were standing in a straight row on the floor, like a class at school, facing their master, an old, long-bearded priest squatting on a mat before the altar.

As we entered, they were wagging their heads in unison, keeping time to a chant monotoned by the old priest. They were of all ages; fat and lean, smooth-shaven and bearded; some in rich garments, others in more sombre and cheaper stuffs.

One face cut itself into my memory, — that of a handsome, clear-skinned young man, with deep, intense eyes and a sinewy, graceful body. On one of his delicate, lady-white hands was a large turquoise ring. Yapouly whispered to me that he was the son of the high priest, and would succeed his father when the old man died.

The chant continued, rising in volume and intensity, and a Nubian in white

64

handed each man a black skull-cap.
These they drew tightly over their perspiring heads.

The movement, which had begun with the slow rolling of their heads, now extended to their bodies. They writhed and twisted as if in agony, — a row of black-capped felons suspended from unseen ropes.

Suddenly there darted out upon the mats a boy scarce ten years of age, spinning like a top, his skirts level with his hands.

The chant broke into a wail, the audience joining in. The howls were deafening. The priest rose from the mats by the altar, slowly waved his hands, and began moving around the room, the worshipers reaching forward and kissing the hem of his robe. As he passed, each dervish stepped one pace forward, and handed his outer robe to the Nubian, who piled them on the floor in front of the altar.

The twelve were now rocking their heads in a wild frenzy, groaning in long, subdued moans, ending in a peculiar "hough," like the sound of a dozen distant locomotives tugging up a steep grade.

" Allah, hou! Allah, hou! Allah, hou!"
—the last word expelled with a jerk.

65

Their eyes were starting from their heads, their parched tongues hanging out, the sweat pouring from their faces. The young priest was livid, with eyes closed, — his body swaying uneasily.

A dozen little children were here handed over the rail to the Nubian, who took them in his arms and laid them in a row, with their faces flattened to the mats. The old priest advanced within a step of the first child, his lips moving in prayer, and stretched his arms above the motionless line of fat, chubby little bodies.

Yapouly Isaac leaned over and whispered, " See, now he bless them."

I raised myself on my feet, to see the better. The Nubian held out his hand to the old priest, who balanced himself for a moment, stepped firmly upon the first child, his bare feet sinking into its soft, yielding flesh, and then walked deliberately across the row of prostrate children. As he passed, each little tot raised its head, watched until the last child had been trampled upon, then sprang up, kissed the old priest's robe, and ran laughing from the room.

The sight now was sickening; the dervishes were in the last stages of exhausted frenzy. The once handsome young priest was ghastly, frothing at

66

the mouth, only the white of his eyes visible, — his voice was thick, his breath almost gone. The others were drooping, with knees bent, hardly able to stand.

Suddenly the priest turned his back, prostrated himself before the altar, and prayed silently. The whirling child sank to the ground. The line of dervishes grew still, tottered along the floor, clutched at the hanging curtain, and staggered into the sunlight.

I forced my way along the closely packed aisle, and rushed into the open air. The sight that met my eye stunned me; my breath stopped short. In the midst of the court stood the Nubian serving coffee, the howlers crowding about him, clamoring for cups, and panting for breath like a team of athletes in from a foot-race. I looked for my young priest with the turquoise ring. He was sitting on a bench, rolling a cigarette, his face wreathed with smiles !

And yet the Mohammedan priest, despite his fanaticism, is really a most delightful companion. His tastes are refined, his garments spotless, his man-
67

ners easy and graceful, and his whole bearing distinguished by a repose that is superb, — the repose of unlimited idleness dignified by unquestioned religious authority.

I remember one in particular who spent a morning with me, — a noble old patriarch, dressed in a delicate egg-shell-colored robe that floated about his feet as he walked, an under-garment of mauve, with waist sash of pale blue, and a snow-drift of silk on his head. For four broiling hours, with only such shade as a half-withered plane-tree could afford, did this majestic old fellow, with slippers tucked under him, sit and drink in every movement of my brush. When I had finished, he arose, saluted me after the manner of his race, and pointing first to the sketch, and then to the glistening mosque, said, in the softest of voices : —

"Good dragoman, tell your master I have for him a very great respect. He has opened my eyes to many beautiful things. I am sure he is a most learned man," and passed on with the dignity and composure of a Doge.

Everywhere else did I find this same spontaneous, generous courtesy and kindly good-humor. Only once was I rebuffed. It was in the open plaza of

the Valedé. I had been watching the
shifting scene, following eagerly the
little dabs of color hurrying over the
heated pavement, when my eye fell
upon a cobbler but a few yards off, peg-
ging away at an upturned shoe.   When
my restless pencil had fastened his fez
upon his head, and linked his body to
his three-legged stool, a laugh broke
out among the bystanders crowded
about me, one jovial old Turk calling out
to the unconscious model.   In a moment he was on his feet, forcing his
way through the throng behind me.
Then a hand clutched my shoulder, and
the next instant a wet leather sole was
thrust forward and ground into my paper, spoiling the sketch.

It took five minutes of my most
subtle Oriental diplomacy, sweetened
with several cups of the choicest Turkish coffee, to convince this indignant
shoemaker that I meant no offense.
When I had succeeded, he was so pro-
fuse in his apologies that I had to
smoke a chibouque with him, at his expense, to restore his equanimity.

And yet, under all the courtesy and
good-nature I found everywhere, I could
not help noticing that a certain disquiet
and nervous fear permeated all classes,
—priests and people alike. The gov-

ernment's extreme poverty and constant watchfulness are two things the inhabitant never forgets,—one concerns his taxes, the other his liberty. This fear is so great that many public topics worn threadbare by most Europeans are never whispered by a Turk to his most intimate friend. Even my dear friend and confidential adviser, Mr. Yapouly, finds now and then a subject upon which he is silent. One day I asked him who had been suspected of murdering the predecessor of the present Sultan, and why it had been thought necessary to remove that luxurious son of the Prophet. It was an idle question on my part, and one I supposed anybody in Constantinople could answer; especially so learned and versatile a dragoman as Mr. Yapouly. To my surprise he made no reply : we were in Pera at the time, he preceding me with the trap. When we reached the long cemetery, he stopped, looked carefully over the low wall, as if fearing the very graves, and then said, in his broken conglomerate, too shattered to reproduce here :—

"Effendi, you must not ask such questions. Everybody is a spy: the man asleep on the sofa in the hotel, the waiter behind your chair, the barber who shaves you. Some night your bed

70

will be empty.   Nobody ever asks such
questions in Constantinople."

Nor is this unrest confined to the people.   I noticed the same anxious look on the Sultan's face the day of the *salemlik*—the day he drives publicly to the little mosque to pray, the mosque outside the palace gates.   His face was like that of the acrobat riding bareback at the circus hoop—glad to be through.

But I am in Constantinople to paint, not to moralize, and these glimpses of the treacherous, deadly stream that flows beneath Turkish life are not to my liking.   I want only the gay flowers above its banks and the soft summer air on my cheek, the tall grasses waving in the sunlight, and the glow and radiance of it all.   So, if you please, we will go back to my mosque, and my delightful old priests, and the Greek who sells me grapes and weighs them in a pair of teetering scales, and my caïque with the pew cushion over the bottom, and the big caïkjis, with the chest of a Hercules and the legs of a satyr, who rows my Oriental gondola, and all the beautiful patches of color, fretted arch, and slender column that make life enchanting in this lotus-eating land ; and even to Mr. Yapouly, Mr. Dreco Yapouly, who tells me he has reformed, and will never lie more, "so help him," — Mr. Dreco Isaacs Yapouly, who has lately ceased his unanswered appeals to the gods, and who has left off all his evil ways.

But then I remember that I cannot go back to my old life now, for the summer is ended. Last night there was a great storm of wind and a deluge of rain, the first for four months. All the gold-dust has been washed from the trees and the grasses. The plaza of the Valedé is scoured clean. The little waves around the Galata no longer lap their tongues indolently about the soggy, rotten floats, but snap angrily in the bleak wind. The doors of the mosques are closed, and outside, in the early morning, groups of natives are huddled over charcoal pans. The winter is creeping on apace, and I must be gone. Besides, they are waiting for me at Florian's on the Piazza in my beloved Venice; those scoffers with their cerise and Chianti and *grandi* of Munich beer. Waiting, not to mock, but to kotow, to bend the ear and genuflect, now that my portfolio is bursting, and to say, "Come, let us see your stuff!" and "How the devil did you get away with so much?"

So one morning I tell Isaac to pack my trap, and this time to slip it inside its leather traveling-case, and to get me

72

a "hamal," a human burro — an Arme-
nian, perhaps — who will toss my trunk,
with the extra canvases now all filled,
upon his back, and never break trot
until he dumps it at the station two
miles away.

I instantly detect, in spite of our
close intimacy, an expression of relief
wrinkling Mr. Yapouly's tobacco-colored
countenance. He sighs his regrets, but
with a lightness that shows his heart is
not in them. He has been but a "ha-
mal" himself, he thinks, lugging the trap
about in the heat, and sitting for hours
doing nothing — absolutely nothing.
And I have bought so little in the bazaars, and his commissions are so small.
But then, as he reflects, is he not the
dragoman of dragomans, and might not
future wayfarers be my intimate friends
and his special prey? So he becomes
doubly solicitous as the time draws near.
Would effendi allow him to place a few
pounds of grapes in the compartment,
the road to Philippopolis is so dusty and
the water is so bad? Had not the umbrella better go above, and the rugs on
the other seat?

Last of all, with a certain tenderness
that he knows will appeal to me, where
will the most gracious effendi permit
him to place the dear old trap, my com-

73

panion over so many thousand miles of travel? At my feet? No; on the cushion beside me!

The guard blows his whistle; the carriage doors are locked. Yapouly — Dreco Yapouly, the reformed — leans outside. I move to the window for a parting word. After all, I may have misjudged him. He starts forward, and presses some cards into my hand.

"For your friends, effendi, when they want good dragoman."

I turn up their white faces.

They are clean and newly printed, and bear this inscription : —

Isaac Isaacs,

Dragoman and Interpreter,

Constantinople.

IV. AN ESCAPADE IN COR-DOVA

HE first day he contented himself with merely glancing my way as I emerged from the door of my lodging, following me with his eyes until I disappeared around the corner of the narrow street that leads to the Moorish mosque.

Then he took to raising his hat with quite the air of a hidalgo, standing uncovered on the narrow sidewalk until I passed, expressing by this simple courtesy a sort of silent apology for occupying my premises.

I always returned his salute, wishing him "good day" with great gusto, adding occasionally the desire that the good God would go with him during its sultry hours. Such graceful compliments tend to make life more enjoyable in old Spanish cities.

But he never addressed a word to me in reply, only bowed the lower, his eyes fixed upon mine, his whole manner suggestive of a wistful desire for closer acquaintanceship. To this was added a

75

certain fearless independence which
banished at once all thought of offering
him alms.

I began to wonder who this very courteous, very silent, and very friendly
young man might be. I began also to
count over the various possible and im-
possible motives which might influence
him to become a fixture on the right
of my doorstep every morning when I
started out with my empty sketch-trap.

It was plainly evident that he belonged to the better class of Spaniards,
and not to "the people." You could
see that in his finely chiseled features,
and in the way his clothes, though
slightly the worse for wear, fitted his
graceful, slender figure. You saw it
also in his winning mouth, full of white
teeth, shaded by a dark mustache with
just enough curl to suggest the Don
Juan, — ready for fan, slipper, or blade.
And yet with all this there was a certain
air of sadness about him that enlisted
your sympathy at sight.

The swarthy landlady who peered
through the lattice-blinds had never
seen him before, and expressed, rather
pointedly, I thought, the hope that she
never would again. The picador who
during the bull-fights occupied a room
on the floor above mine charged down

upon him very much as he would on a wounded bull, and returned to me, waiting behind the half-open door, with a shrug of his broad shoulders, a lifting of his eyebrows, and the single word, " Nada !" ("Good-for-nothing ").

Still the silent young man continued to occupy my sidewalk, to bow with his hat to the ground, and to follow me with his eyes around the corner of the narrow street that led to the Moorish mosque.

Then a break occurred in the daily programme. I had forgotten my brush-case, and ran back into the house, leaving my white umbrella and trap on the doorstep. When I emerged again into the blinding sunlight they had disappeared. I instinctively sought out my silent young man. He was standing in his customary place, hat off, my trap in one hand, — the umbrella under his arm.

" My friend, you have my trap."

" Yes, señor."

" Why ?"

" It is too heavy for the painter. Let me carry it."

His voice was so gentle, his face so honest, his manner so courteous, his desire to serve me so apparent, that I surrendered the brush-case at once; had it been filled with doubloons I would have done the same.

"What is your name?"

"Manuel."

"Why are you always here?"

"To wait upon you."

"For what?"

"To keep from starving."

"Have you had any breakfast?"

"No; nor supper."

Below the mosque there runs a crooked street lined with balconies hooded with awnings shading tropical plants, and now and then a pretty señorita. At the end of this street is an arcade flanking the old bull-ring. Through one of its arches you enter the best café in Cordova.

To see a hungry man eat has always been to me one of the most delightful of all the expositions of the laws of want and supply; to assist in equalizing these laws the most exquisite of pleasures. I exhausted all my resources on Manuel.

He had a cup of coffee as big as a soup-bowl. He had an omelet crammed full of garlic. He had a pile of waffles smothered in sugar. He had chicken livers broiled in peppers and little round radishes, and a yard of bread, and, last of all, a flagon of San Vicente. All

78

these he ate and drank with the air and manners of a gentleman, smoking a cigarette, as is the custom, throughout the entire repast, and talking to me of his life, — his people at home, his year at the military school at Toledo, of the unfortunate scrape which ended in his dismissal, of the anger of his father, of the beauty and devotion of the girl who caused it all, and of his coming to Cordova to be near her. Who does not recollect his own shortcomings in the hot, foolish days of his youth ? I could see it all ; hardly twenty, straight as an arrow, lithe as a whip, eyes coals of fire, cheeks like a rose, and his veins packed full of blood at fever-heat.

He had watched me painting in the plaza, and had followed me to my lodgings, hoping I would employ him to carry my trap, but had been too timid to ask for it until chance threw it in his way. He would be glad to carry it now all day to pay for his breakfast.

Manuel was a prize. He would supply the only thing I lacked in this most charming of Spanish cities, — a boon companion with nothing to do. I made a bargain with him on the spot, — so many pesetas per week, with three meals a day, he to occupy the other side of the table.

79

It was delightful to see him when the terms were concluded. His face lighted up, and his big brown eyes danced. Now he could hold up his head. His father perhaps was right, but what could he do? Florita was so lovely! Some day I should see her; but not now; I would not understand. His father by and by would relent and send for him. Then he would take my hand and place it in his father's and say, "Here is the good painter who saved my life and Florita's."

We ransacked Cordova from end to end: into the mosque at twilight, sitting in the shadows of the forest of marble columns stretching away on every side; up into the tower, where the pigeons roost; across the old Roman bridge; along the dusty highways on the outskirts of the old city crowded with market people; through the streets at night, listening to the tinkling of guitars and watching the muffled figures under the balconies, and the half-opened lattices with the little hands waving handkerchiefs or dropping roses; everywhere and anywhere; in every nook and crack and cranny of this once famous home of the hidalgo, the cavalier, and the inamorata with the eyes of a gazelle and the heart of fire.

Manuel loved it all. He loved, too, strange to say, all things quaint and odd and old, and in his enthusiasm had rummaged every sacristy and priest's house for me in search of such treasures. Indeed, there was hardly a purchasable vestment or bit of embroidery in the city that he had not bargained for, and my lodgings gave daily evidence of his success. One morning he came dancing in, bubbling over with delight, and swinging around his head a piece of brocade that would have made the mouth of an antiquary water. This he gravely informed me had once belonged to the figure of the good saint, the Santa Teresa, who had worn it for some hundreds of years, and who had parted with it the night before for ten pesetas. The sacristan who acted as her agent had replaced the exquisite relic with some new, cheap lace, explaining that it was the good saint's feast-day, and he was therefore especially desirous of presenting her properly to her devout admirers.

One subject, however, by common silent consent was tabooed, — the whereabouts of the sweetheart who had made him an exile. I knew that she was young, graceful as a doe, seductive as a houri, and beautiful beyond compare. I knew that she loved Manuel wildly,

81

that he idolized her, and would starve rather than desert her. I knew also that she lived within a stone's-throw of the café ; for Manuel would leave me at breakfast to kiss her good-morning, and at midday to kiss her again, and at sundown to kiss her once more good-night, and would return each time within ten minutes. I knew also, of course, that her name was Florita. All this the young fellow told me over and over again, with his face flushed and his eyes aflame ; but I knew nothing more.

One night of each week was always Manuel's. Any part of any other night, or all of it, for that matter, was mine, and he was at my service for sight-seeing or prowling ; but Saturday was Florita's.

Except on festival nights, Saturday, of all nights in the week, is the gayest in all the Spanish cities. Then the cafés are in full blast, filled not only with the city people, but with the country folk who come to market on that day. These cafés have raised platforms, are edged by a row of footlights, and hold half a dozen chairs seating as many male and female dancers. Here you see on gala nights the most bewitching of all the sights of Spain, — the Spanish dancers.

What music is to the Italian, dancing
is to the Spaniard. Float along through any of the canals of Venice and listen : everybody is singing. The woman in the window of the wine-shop over the way is humming an air from Trovatore. The idler on the quay joins in the melody, and in five minutes more the whole waterway is ringing with its sublime harmony. Turn out into the Grand Canal and so on into the Lido. The boats from Chioggia, fish-laden, are drifting up to the marble front of the Public Garden, and the air is filled with the pathos of some refrain a hundred years old. It is the language of the people ; they think, talk, vibrate in music.

In Spain the outlet is through the toes, and not only through the toes, but the feet, the ankles, legs, up and through the spinal column, out along the arms to the very finger-tips, every nerve, tissue, muscle, and drop of blood in their swinging, pulsating bodies tingling to the rhythm of the dance. Under the influence of this magic spell a man with one eye and a crooked leg, head bound with a red handkerchief, jacket and waistcoat off, will transform himself into an embodiment of grace and expression. He will give you whole columns of description with his legs,

83

avenge the forlorn heroine with the
small of his back, and deal death and
destruction to the villain with a twist of
his head. It is the condensation of the
opera, the drama, the pantomime, and
the story - teller. Pictures, harmonies,
books, the platform, and the footlights
have their own well-worn roads to your
brain ; this language of the toes ploughs
a furrow of its own.

On this particular Saturday night
Manuel had taken himself off as usual,
and I was left to follow my own free
will alone. So I strolled into the garden of the mosque, sat me down on one
of the stone seats under the orange-
trees, and watched the women fill their
water-jars at the old Moorish well, listening meanwhile to the chatter of their
gossip. When it grew quite dark, I
passed out through the Puerta del Per-
don, turned to the right, and wandered
on aimlessly down a narrow street leading to the river. Soon I heard the click
of castanets and the thrum of guitars.
There was a dance somewhere. Pushing aside a swinging door, I entered a
small café.

The room was low-ceiled, apparently
without windows, and the air stifling.
The customary stage occupied one corner of the interior, which was crowded

84

to the very walls with water-carriers, cargadors, gypsies, hucksters, and the young bloods of the town. They were cheering wildly a black-eyed señorita who had just finished her dance, and who was again at the footlights bowing her acknowledgments. She made a pretty picture in her short yellow skirts trimmed with black, her high comb, and her lace mantilla, her bare arms waving gracefully. I found a seat near the door, called for a bottle of San Vicente, and lighted a cigarette. At the adjoining table sat a group of young fellows drinking aguardiente. It is a villainous liquor, and more than a thimbleful sets a man's brain on fire. They were measuring theirs in tumblers. When at a second recall the girl again refused to dance, the manager explaining that she was very tired, the young caballeros began pounding the table with their glasses, shouting out in angry tones, " La señorita ! la señorita ! " When for the third time the young girl advanced to the platform's edge and bowed her regrets, one of the group sprang forward, leaped upon a table, and with an oath dashed the contents of his glass over her bare shoulders. A frightened shriek cut the air, and the next instant a heavy carafe filled with wine grazed my head, struck the

85

ruffian full in the face, and tumbled him headlong to the floor.

Instantly the place was in an uproar. Half a dozen men, one waving an ugly knife, sprang past me, made a rush for the table in my rear, and threw themselves upon a young fellow who had thrown the carafe, and who stood with his back to me swinging its mate over his head like a flail. Then came a crash, another Spaniard sprawled on the floor, and a flying figure dashed by and bounded over the footlights. As he plunged through the curtain in the rear I caught sight of his face. It was Manuel!

Grasping the situation, I sprang through the door and reached the sidewalk just as the police forced their way past me into the scattering throng. A few sharp orders, a crash of breaking glass, a rattling of carbines on the floor, and the tumult was over.

Humiliated at Manuel's deception, and yet anxious for his safety, I hid myself in the shadow near a street lamp, with my eye on the swinging door, and waited. The first man thrust out was the ruffian who had emptied his glass over the dancer. His arms were pinioned behind his back, his head still bloody from the effects of Manuel's carafe. Then came a villainous-looking cut-throat with a gash across his cheek, followed by three others, one of whom was the manager.

The mob surrounded the group, the prisoners in front. I crouched close until they disappeared in a body up the street, then crossed over, and swung back the door. The place was empty. A man in his shirt-sleeves was putting out the lights.

"There has been a row?" I said.

"Unquestionably."

"And some arrests?"

"Yes, señor."

"Did they get them all?"

"All but one."

"Where is he?"

The man stopped, grinned the width of his face, and, thrusting up his thumb, waved it meaningly over his left shoulder.

Manuel had escaped!

For half the night I brooded over the unfaithfulness of human nature. Here was my hero telling lies to me about his Florita, spending his Saturday nights in a low café engaged in vulgar brawls, and all over a dancer. I began to consider and doubt. Was there any such fair creature at all as Florita? Was there any implacable father? Had Manuel ever been a student? Was it not all

a prearranged scheme to bleed me day
by day and, awaiting a chance, rob me,
or worse? A man who could escape un-
hurt, surrounded as he had been, was no
ordinary man. Perhaps he was simply
a decoy for one of the numerous bands
of brigands still infesting the mountains; and I remembered with a shudder the story about the forefinger of the
Englishman forwarded to his friends in
a paper box as a sort of sight draft on
his entire bank account. I began to
bless myself that mere accident had
warned me in time. I would pick up
no more impecunious tramps, with my
heart and pocketbook wide open.

When the day broke, and the cheery
sun that Manuel always loved streamed
in my windows, the situation seemed to
improve. I thought of his open, honest
face, of his extreme kindness and grati-
tude, of the many delightful hours we
had spent together. Perhaps, after all,
it was not Manuel. I saw his face only
for a moment, and these Spaniards are
so much alike, all so dark and swarthy.
He would surely come in an hour, and
we would have our coffee together. I
dragged a chair out on the balcony and
sat down, watching anxiously the turn
of the street where I had so often
caught sight of him waving his hand.

88

At eight o'clock I gave him up. It was true; the face was Manuel's, and he dared not show himself now for fear of arrest. Then a new thought cheered me. Perhaps he was waiting at the café, or, it being Sunday, was late, and I would meet him on the way. How could I have misjudged him so. Filled with these thoughts I ran downstairs into the sunlight and stopped at the corner near the church, scanning the street up and down. There was no one I knew except the old bareheaded beggar with the withered arm. Manuel often gave him alms. He bowed as I passed, stood up, and put on his hat.

Near the café at the bottom of the hill stands a half-ruined archway. It can be reached by two streets running parallel and within a stone's-throw of each other. As I passed under this arch, the beggar, to my astonishment, started up as if from the ground. He had followed me.

"You are the painter, señor?"

"Yes."

"And Manuel's friend?"

"Of course; where is he?"

He glanced cautiously about, drew me under the shadow of the wall, and took a scrap of paper from inside the band of his hat.

It bore this inscription :—

"I am in trouble; follow the beggar."

The old man looked at me fixedly, turned sharply, and retraced his steps through the arch. My decision was instantaneous ; I would find Manuel at all hazards.

The way led across the plaza of the bull-ring, through the fruit-market, up the hill past the little mosque, — now the church of Santa Maria, the one with the red marble altar, — and so on out into the suburbs of the city, the beggar keeping straight ahead and never looking behind. At the end of a narrow lane dividing two rows of old Moorish houses the mendicant tarried long enough for me to come quite near, glanced at me meaningly, and then disappeared in a crack in the wall. I followed, and found myself in a square patio, overgrown with weeds, half choked by the ruins of a fountain, and surrounded by a balcony supported by marble columns. This balcony was reached by a stone staircase. The beggar crossed the overgrown tangle, mounted the steps, swung back a heavy green door with Moorish hinges, and waited for me to pass in.

I drew back. The folly, if not the

danger, of the whole proceeding began to dawn upon me.

"I will go no farther. Where is the man who sent you?"

The beggar placed his fingers to his lips and pointed behind him.

At the same instant a blind opened cautiously on the floor above, and Manuel's face, pale as a ghost, peered through the slats. The beggar entered, closed the heavy door carefully, felt his way along a dark corridor, and knocked twice. A shriveled old woman with a bent back thrust out her head, mumbled something to the beggar, and led me to an opening in the opposite wall. Manuel sprang out and seized my hand.

"I knew you would come. Oh, such a scrape! The police searched for us half the night. But for old Bonta, the beggar here, and his wife we would have been caught. It would kill my father if anything should happen now. See, here is his letter saying we can come home! Oh, I am so grateful to you! You see it was this way. It was Florita's night, and I" —

My heart turned sick within me. Florita's night! If the poor girl only knew!

"Don't say another word, Manuel;

you are in a scrape, and I will help you out, but don't lie about it to me of all men. If you love the dancer, all right. Breaking a carafe over a fellow's head in a café, and all for a pair of ankles, may be " —

"Lie to you, señor!" said Manuel, flushing angrily, and with a certain dignity I had never seen in him before ; "I could never lie to you. You do not know."

"I do know."

"Then Bonta has told you?" and he looked towards the beggar.

"Bonta has not opened his lips. I saw it all with my own eyes, and you may thank your lucky stars that you were not sliced full of holes. What would Florita say?"

"Florita? Jesu, I see!" said Manuel, springing forward, pushing open the door, and calling out :—

"Florita! Are you there? Come quick!"

A hurried step in the adjoining room, and a young girl came running in.

It was the dancer!

"What could I do, señor? What would you do if your own wife had been so insulted? See how lovely she is!" And he kissed her on both cheeks.

What would I have done? What

would you have done, my friend, with that startled shriek in your ears, her great eyes wet with tears, her white arms held out to you?

My hair is not quite so brown as it was, and the blood no longer surges through my veins. I am cooler and calmer, and even phlegmatic; and yet had Florita been mine, I would have broken a carafe over every head in Cordova.

While he was calming her fears, kissing her cheeks, and patting her hands, the whole story came out. Day after day he had hoped that his father would relent. One word from him, and then I need never have known how the dainty feet of his pretty young wife had helped them both to live.

That night, a painter, with a pretty Spanish cousin, and a servant carrying his coat and trap, occupied a first-class carriage for Toledo.

The painter left the train at the first station out of Cordova, shouldered his trap and coat himself, and took the night express back to his lonely lodgings. The servant and the señorita went on alone.

When the train reached Toledo, an old Spaniard with white head and mustache pushed his way through the crowd, took

93

the servant in his arms, and kissed the
pretty cousin on both cheeks.

Then a high-springed old coach swallowed them all up.

V. LA CÁNAL DE LA VIGA

T begins at the great lakes, away up in the country among the flowers and market gardens, winds in and out of the low hills and hollows, stopping at the various Aztec towns with the unpronounceable names. Then it takes a turn into the little holiday village of Santa Anita where the flower-crowned peons dance feast-days and Sundays, waters the edges of the *chinampas,*— the floating gardens of the ancients overgrown with weeds and anchored by neglect, —flows past the almost deserted *paseo de la Viga*, holding half-way its length the dilapidated bust of Guatimotzin, and so on down to the City of Mexico.

All kinds of water-craft loaded with all kinds of merchandise float up and down its windings : wood boats ; market boats ; flower boats ; canoes filled with Indians ; flat-bottomed barges roofed over with a rude awning amidships, — barbaric gondolas, crowded with merrymakers thrumming guitars and clicking

95

castanets, — a steady stream of life, with the current towards the city.

Here it is swallowed up like many another fresh young life joyous from the green fields. Here the city pounces upon it and defiles it. Here every bit of stray refuse, every scrap of offal, all the filth, all the dirt, all the scrapings and castaways of the great city are thrust into its pure waters. Even the narrow little bridges take a hand in the villainy; crowding and jostling as if bent on choking it up forever.

Soon it reaches the slums, the very dregs of its pollution; the stables; the dyehouses and the sewers; the slaughter-houses, where the brown-backed peons, naked to the waist, lean over rotting logs cleansing the reeking hides fresh from the shambles. Every indignity is heaped upon it, every touch befouls it.

Still it struggles on, cringing like an outcast, slinking under the bridges, crouching through dark waterways, edging along rotting embankments, buoyed up and strengthened by the thought of the bright pure waters of Lake Texcoco glistening in the sunlight a few miles away.

You follow down, in and out, crossing and recrossing the little bridges, hugging the shadows of the tall pink and La Canal de la Viga yellow washed buildings, — their balco- nies trellised with flowers and hooded with awnings, — until you come to where the water widens out, washing a broad flight of stone steps that lead up to four great columns supporting the entabla- ture and roof of an imposing structure quite classic in its design. This is the Mercado del Pulquerria.

Cross the little bridge above, pick your way through the crowds of venders in the street, push through the babel of buyers and sellers on the floor of the market, and walk out into the blinding sunlight on the very same stone steps you saw from across the canal. A sight greets you that exists only in one spot the world over.

Beneath, in a solid pack, their sides touching, floats a great fleet of canoes loaded to the water's edge with masses of flowers, heaps of vegetables, piles upon piles of fruit : — one solid carpet of blue larkspur, bright marigolds and car- nations, poppies, roses, radishes, lettuce, tomatoes, melons, grapes, and figs.

You forget the ninety and nine smells, the seething, bubbling hides, the ooze and slime of the sodden logs, and revel only in the sunlight, the palms waving over the low walls, the blazing, dazzling

97

white of the great building opposite, the deep blue of the sky overhead, and the superb carpet of color dotted with figures beneath.

Stand behind one of the great pillars within a few feet of the nearest boat. Its bow is a mass of blue larkspur and ragged sailors. Amidships is a great square of carnations, intermingled with every variety of reds and yellows. In the stern stands a peon girl, her head covered by a wide-peaked sombrero of yellow straw, throwing the richly colored face in shadow.

The sunlight falls on her bare arms and back, and glistens on the white chemise, half concealing the full outlines of her rounded figure. About her hips is folded a square, blue cotton blanket, girded by a red sash. In her ears are large silver hoops. An armlet of copper binds one arm near the shoulder.

She stands erect, steadying herself, — one hand on the oar, which in turn steadies the boat, the other filled with fruit and flowers. These she lifts up to the clamoring crowd, tossing them now a bunch of radishes, now a cluster of carnations in exchange for their copper coins, which she catches dexterously in mid-air.

If you think grace died with the

Greeks, watch this girl for a moment. *La Canal de la Viga* She is barely sixteen ; her eyes are dark and luminous ; her hair a purple black, tied in two great braids down her back ; her teeth white as milk ; her neck, arms, and bust exquisitely modeled ; her fingers small and tapering, and her feet tiny enough to dance on Persian carpets. She has a skin that is not the red of the Indian, nor brown, nor quadroon ; it is light though transparent copper.

Every movement is grace itself. That she comes of an indolent race only adds to her beauty. Minutes at a time she keeps perfectly still, even to her eyelids. Then she shifts the oar, throws her weight on the other hip, her beautiful bare arms fall to her side, and she is more entrancing than ever. She is absolutely unconscious of your admiration. She has but one thought in life, — to sell her cargo before the hot sun shall shrivel it up.

Suddenly, above the din of the traffic, you hear a sharp cry. The girl starts forward, drops the oar and falls on her knees in the boat, among the greens and flowers. When she rises she has her little bare, bronze baby in her arms.

At the same instant, from underneath, there crawls out a shaggy-headed peon rubbing his eyes. He has been sound

99

asleep. Long before the gray dawn, and many weary miles from here, he had poled the canoe alone; past the sleeping villages and the *chinampas*, while the mother and child rested.

The crowd thins out. One by one the boats drop off, and drift up or down. Soon the bronze goddess and her baby and her shaggy-headed husband float by with an empty boat.

You look after them long and musingly, until they are lost in the throng. Then, somehow, you feel a slight pain, as of a personal loss. The place is different, the charm has fled.

You begin to note the foul water strewn with waste leaves, decayed fruit, and the offal of the market. You become aware of the stench and the reeking filth. The white wall glows like a furnace, — the sky is molten brass, — the palms hang limp. You turn in disgust and enter the stifling market, where barelegged peons are drenching the foul stone flags with fouler water from the canal, and so on through and out into the narrow street, dodging under the awnings, and skirting close to the strip of a black shadow stenciled on the sidewalk.

Soon you reach your garden, and the cool of your quiet siesta.

Over your coffee you have but one *La Canal* memory, — the grand figure of that *de la Viga* daughter of Montezuma, radiant in the sunlight, her hands filled with flowers.

VI. A BULGARIAN OPERA BOUFFE

E was a small waiter with a slightly bald head, and of no very pronounced nationality, and he spoke the fag-ends of five or six languages, one of which, I was delighted to find, was my own.

These fragments he hurled continuously at other waiters of more pronounced nationalities — French, German, Hungarian, and the like — who were serving little groups of Turks, Russians, and Bulgarians scattered about the coffee-room.

Directly opposite me hung a half-length portrait of a broad-shouldered young soldier bristling with decorations, his firmly set features surmounted by a military cap.

"Is that a portrait of the prince?" I asked.

The man of many tongues stopped, looked at the chromo for an instant as though trying to remember to which one of the late princes I had referred, and then said blandly : —

"Yes, monsieur; the present king; Prince Ferdinand."

"Is he now in Sofia?"

The slightly bald attendant elevated his eyebrows with a look of profound astonishment.

"Here? No, monsieur."

"He has really run away, then?"

The eyebrows fell, and a short, pudgy finger was laid warningly against his lips.

"Monsieur, nobody runs in Bulgaria. His majesty is believed to be in the monastery at Ryllo."

"Yes, so they tell me. But will he ever come back here?"

The man stopped, gazed about him furtively, refilled my glass, bending so low that his lips almost touched my ear, and then whispered, with a half-laugh:

"God knows."

I was not surprised. All Europe at that precise moment was straining its ears to catch a more definite answer. The conundrum was still going the rounds of the diplomats, and the successful guesser was yet to be heard from.

All that was positively known concerning his imperial highness was that several weeks prior to the time of this writing he had left his palace at Sofia, the capital of Bulgaria, — within mus-

ket-shot of where I sat, — and, attended
by a few personal friends, had taken the
midnight express to Vienna. From Vienna he had gone to Carlsbad, where
for several consecutive weeks he had
subjected his royal person to as many
indoor baths and as much outdoor ex-
ercise as would entirely eradicate the
traces of gout and other princely evils
absorbed by his kingship during his few
years' stay in the capital of the Bulgarians.

All this time the air had been full of
the rumor of his abdication. The Russian ambassador at the court of Paris,
Baron Mohrenheim, in an interview
granted to the Paris correspondent of a
St. Petersburg paper, insisted that there
was no doubt that Ferdinand had quitted Bulgaria for good, "his life there
being in constant danger." While the
Austrian ambassador at Constantinople,
Herr von Radowitz, was reported to
have advised the Porte to postpone taking action on the Bulgarian Note for the
present, hinting at the imminent retire-
ment of the reigning prince, and a consequent solution of impending difficulties more in harmony with the purport
of the Berlin Treaty.

These announcements continued, and
with such persistency that the Bulgarian

prime minister, M. Stamboloff, deemed it necessary to telegraph to a newspaper correspondent, "The rumors of the prince's intended abdication are pure fabrications."

More emphatic still was Ferdinand's own manifesto, issued through the columns of the Carlsbad "Temps," to the effect that "while there is a great national effervescence going on at this moment in Bulgaria, the Bulgarians are, nevertheless, free, and will welcome me back with rejoicings."

It was while this political "effervescence," as the prince was pleased to call it, continued that the royal liver grew torpid enough to demand a change of air. This torpidity lasted, in fact, long after the Carlsbad doctors had pronounced the diseased organ cured. You will remember that Talleyrand tried the same experiment with similar results nearly a century before.

Then one day the prince turned up serenely on the slopes of the mountains, dismounted like a weary knight, and knocked for admission at the monastery at Ryllo.

Being myself a wanderer in this part of the world, with an eye for the unexpected and the picturesque, and anxious to learn the exact situation in Bulgaria, I had hurried on from Budapest, and at high noon on a broiling August day had arrived at a way station located in the midst of a vast sandy plain. This station the conductor informed me was Sofia. Following my traps through a narrow door guarded by a couple of soldiers, I delivered up my ticket and passport, crept under a heap of dust propped up on wheels and drawn by three horses abreast with chair‑backs over their hames, waited until a Turk, two greasy Roumanians, — overcoated in sheepskins wrong side out, — and a red‑neck-tied priest had squeezed in beside me; and then started off in a full gallop to a town two miles away. Our sudden exodus obliterated the station in a cloud of dust, through which the Constantinople express could be seen slowly feeling its way.

The interview with the waiter occurred within an hour of my arrival.

The same afternoon I was abroad in the streets of Sofia armed with such information as I had gathered from my

In the king's absence I would call upon the members of the cabinet.

It did not take me many hours to discover that his Excellency M. Stamboloff, Minister President, was away on a visit, presumably at Philippopolis; that the Minister of Justice, M. Salabashoff, had resigned a short time before; that Doctor Stransky, Minister of Foreign Affairs, had followed suit, the portfolios of both being still unassigned; that the Minister of Finance was in Varna, the Minister of War, Colonel Moutkourov, in Vienna. In fact, that not a single member of the Bulgarian government from the king down was to be found at the capital. The Bulgarian government had apparently absconded. Not a member, not a representative, was to be found, unless a gimlet-eyed man of about forty, with a forbidding countenance, a flat military cap, and a tight-fitting white surtout incrusted with gilt buttons, who answered as prefect of police, might be so considered.

I ran up against this gentleman before I quitted the palace grounds. He had already run up against me at the station on my arrival, — as I afterward discovered, — and had entered me as a suspicious character at sight.

In five minutes he had bored me so full of questions that I became as transparent as my passport, which he held up to the light in order to read its water-mark. Next he went through my sketch-book page by page, and finally through all my letters until he came to one bearing at its top the image of the American eagle and at its bottom the superscription of one of its secretaries, answering for my sobriety, honesty, and industry; whereupon he waved me to the door with full permission to roam and sketch at my will. Then he put a special detective on my track, who never took his eyes from me during any one of my waking hours.

I did not ask this potentate whether the prince was coming back. I did not consider it an opportune moment.

Neither did I discuss with him the present condition of Bulgaria, there being nothing in the cut of his coat — nor of his eye, for that matter — to indicate his present political views. He might have been an adherent of the prince, or a believer in Panitza, or a minion of Stamboloff, or he might have been so evenly balanced on the edge of events as to be all three or none.

Nor did I explain to him how grieved I was that his present lords and masters should have seen fit to absent themselves just at the precise moment when their combined presence would have been so agreeable to me. I had really crossed desert wastes to study their complicated comedy, and now all the principal actors were out of town.

A rehearsal of the preceding acts of this play may possibly lead to a better understanding of the drama as it was then being developed in Bulgaria. It is not heroic; it cannot even be called romantic, this spectacle in which three millions of souls are seen hunting about Europe for a sovereign, — a sort of still-hunt resulting in the capture of two kings in four years, with hopes of bagging a protector or a president before the fifth is out.

But to the play itself.

At present in Bulgaria there are, first, the Russophiles, who, as Petko Karaveloff says, "pray for the time when Bulgaria shall march into Salonica, while Russia marches into Constantinople," and who believe the Czar to be their natural friend and ally, with the only

hope of settled peace in his protector-
ate. Secondly, the loyal oppositionists,
headed by M. Radoslavoff, who would
support the prince with certain conces-
sions, but who detest his advisers. And
thirdly, the sympathizers of Major Panitza, the murdered patriot, who was
" shot " — so ran a proclamation a week
old, patches of which were still pointed
out to me decorating the walls of the
king's palace — " by the order of the
bloodthirsty Ferdinand, the scoundrel
Stamboloff, and the 'Vaurien' Moutkourov."

This young officer, Panitza, — a devoted adherent of Prince Alexander, —
had served with distinction in the Ser-
vian war, having led one of the famous
charges at Slivnitza. Believing that the
only salvation for his country lay in Russian interference, he had joined hands
with a Russian spy, Kolobkoff, in fo-
menting discord in the army. Unluckily,
his own letters, carrying unmistakable
evidence of the plot, fell into the hands
of Stamboloff himself, resulting in his
immediate arrest, trial, and condemna-
tion by court-martial.

It is greatly to the credit of Prince
Ferdinand that he was strongly inclined
to spare Panitza. He in fact held out
for more than a week against the com-

bined assaults of Stamboloff and his brother-in-law, Moutkourov, — then minister of war, — and it was not until his prime ministêr threatened the resignation of the entire cabinet that he finally yielded. There is even a story current that when this threat failed Stamboloff followed the king to Lom Palanka with the death-warrant in his hand, and that when he still hesitated that implacable dictator remarked sententiously : —

" Sire, Major Panitza dies on the morrow. If you continue to object, there is one thing we can always do for your majesty, — we can always buy you a first-class ticket to Vienna."

Stamboloff's plan for governing had been simple and to the point. It called for five millions of roubles and a king. Who this king might be, or where he should hail from, was a matter of detail. Anybody but a Russian or a Turk would do. And so offers were made in a confidential way to various gentlemen who thought they had an especial, divine gift for reigning, and who lacked the opportunity only because of the depleted condition of their bank accounts. At last a fond and ambitious mother and an obliging son with an almost unlimited reserve fund — unlimited for the ordinary needs of life — took the bait.

III

It was not, however, a harmonious
family arrangement; for it was well
known that the young prince's uncle,
the Duke of Saxe-Coburg, did what he
could to prevent the final agreement;
he being an older and wiser diplomat,
and having had a long and varied experience in the ups and downs of several
see - saw governments. Among other
things, the duke boldly stated that it
was only a question of money with the
Bulgarian regents, and that Ferdinand
would leave the throne when his guldens
were gone, as had Alexander, to whom
the Bulgarian government then owed
three millions of francs.

The duke was right. When the hour
arrived, there were, of course, cogent
reasons for heavy drafts on the king's
exchequer :— the army was to be re-
armed and clothed, an important railroad built, and a thousand and one improvements made. The money would
be returned.

This schedule has been literally carried out, — except the return item, — if
not to the benefit of Bulgaria herself,
certainly to the depletion of the prince's
bank account.

Among the most seductive of these
schemes was the beautifying of the capital. Streets were to be opened, and

trees planted, and flowers made to bloom.
I recall now that vast band of stagnant
dust leading from the station to the
town, separated from its surrounding
monotony by sundry depressions and
grades indicated along the line by the
excavated débris which fringed its
edges ; with a double row of infant trees
marking its curb-lines, each one of
which was shriveled to a crisp by the
blistering heat. Added to this mockery,
at regular intervals stood flower-beds in
ovals, and diamonds, and circles, filled
with plants burned to a cinder, their
very blossoms, which no man had dared
pluck, dead for months, and still standing brown and dust-begrimed.

Such is the great boulevard leading
from the railway to the palace !

The boulevard, however, is not the
only part of Sofia illustrating the prevailing taste to overturn and recon-
struct. One sees it in the new part of
the town, where government buildings,
bare, white, and forbidding, are going
up in all directions. One sees it also
in the old mosque-and-garden-landmarks
left standing high above new streets
now being cut to their very edges ; their
preservation a tacit acknowledgment
of their right to exist, their isolation a
forerunner of their death, — quite as the

113

old traditions are being undermined by the present government.

Many of these streets serve a double purpose. They make a short route to the palace, and they provide right of way for hasty artillery practice. One cannot always tell, in so changeable a climate as that of Bulgaria, when the prevailing political wind may shift.

The palace itself, a great hospital-looking building surrounded by a garden, suggests only stately discomfort and emptiness. In walking through its great halls and scantily furnished salons, I could not help pondering upon the peculiarities of human nature, and wondering what could have induced this fine young officer — and he is a fine fellow in every sense of the word — to give up his brilliant life in Vienna, the most delightful capital in Europe, and to a young man of fortune the most fascinating, in order to bury himself in this ugly pile of masonry. But then the market is never overstocked with empty thrones, while would-be kings are a drug.

The old part of the town, however, is still quaint and Oriental, and has thus far escaped the restless shovel and saw. It lies in the dip of a saucer-shaped valley, surrounded by bare brown hills. Netted with crooked, dirty streets and

114

choked with low, shambling houses, with here and there a ruined mosque, it remains a picturesque reminder of the days of Turkish rule, unchanged since the signing of the Berlin Treaty, when in a single year five thousand of Mohammed's chosen shook the dust of Sofia from their feet and sought refuge under the Sultan.

The most interesting of these quaint remnants of Oriental architecture found in the old part of the city is the Mosque Bania-bashie, dating back to the year 1279. This mosque is still the resort of the devout Mohammedan, who prays therein five times a day with his face towards Mecca, and who, despite the restrictions that vex his race, still prostrates himself on the floor of the mosque below, in obedience to the call of the muezzin from the slender minaret above.

Here I had my first glimpse of Mohammedan worship, and to one unaccustomed to the forms of the Mohammedan religion, and especially to one who sees them for the first time, I know of no religious spectacle more impressive. Before you stands a barefooted Turk erect on his prayer-rug with his face towards Mecca and his eyes looking straight into the eyes of his God. You see at a glance that it is not a duty with him, nor a formality, nor the main tenance of a time-honored custom. It is his very life. Watch him as he enters this wretched interior of Bania-bashie, with its scaling and crumbling walls, and its broken windows through which the doves fly in and out. Outside, at the trickling fountain, he has washed his feet and face and hands, bathing his throat and smoothing his beard with his wet fingers. He is a rough, broad-shouldered, poorly clad man in fez and skirt, his waist girt with a wide sash ragged and torn. He is perhaps a "ha-mal," a man who carries great weights on his back, — a human beast of burden. His load, whatever it may be, is outside in the court. His hourly task is his daily bread; but he has heard the shrill cry from the minaret up against the sky, and stops instantly to obey.

He enters the sacred building with his shoes in his hands. These he leaves at the edge of the mat. Now he is on holy ground. Advancing slowly, he halts half-way across the floor, and stands erect. Before him is a blank wall; beyond it the tomb of the Pro-phet. For a moment he is perfectly still, his eyes closed, his lips motionless. It is as if he stood in the antechamber of Heaven, awaiting recognition. Then

116

his face lights up. He has been seen! *A Bulga-rian Opera Bouffe*
The next instant he is on his knees,
and, stretching out his hands, prostrates
himself, his forehead pressed to the floor.
This solitary service continues for an
hour. The man stands erect one moment, with a movement as if he said,
"Command me; I am here;" the next
he is prostrate in obedience. Then he
backs slowly out, and, noiseless, regains
his shoes, bends his back to his burden,
and keeps on his way, his face having
lost all its tired, hunted look.

There is no mistaking the impression
made upon you. It is not a religious
ceremony, nor a form of devotion, nor a
prayer. This man has been in the very
presence of his God.

Next to this crumbling mosque stands
the Turkish bath, with its round dome
pierced with bull's-eyes through which
the light falls in slanting parallel bars
upon clouds of boiling steam. The water gushes from the ground at a temper-
ature of 110° Fahrenheit, the pool being
shoulder-deep and filling the whole interior excepting the narrow edge around
which cling the half-boiled natives in
every variety of undress uniform from
the pattern used in the Garden of Eden
down to the modern dressing-gown.

Outside of this circular room are cool-

117

ing apartments smelling of wet towels and furnished with divans upon which men lounge half-clad, smoking cigarettes. Now and then from an inside cubbyhole come the whiff of a narghile and that unmistakable aroma, the steam of smoking coffee.

What a luxury after a four months' drought and its consequent accumulation of Bulgarian dust! How genuine and unique this volcanic-heated symposium compared to all its base imitations palmed off on a suffering public in the several capitals of Europe and America! For more than six hundred years, and in fact before the mosque was built, has this pool of Siloam comforted the sick and soothed the well and cleansed the soiled. And hot, too, — boiling hot out of the ground, running free night and day, and always ready with its accompaniments of Turkish coffee, pipes, and divans. Go to, with your marble slabs, and radiators, and high-pressure boilers under the sidewalk!

Beyond this section of narrow streets there runs a broad highway lined with booths attended by all sorts of peoples — Gypsies, Turks, Jews, Greeks, and Hungarians, selling every kind of merchandise entirely worthless to anybody but a native. Here are rings of bread,

118

squares of leather for sandals, messes in bowls with indescribable things float- ing about in boiling grease, heaps and lumps of other things served smoking hot in wooden plates, and festoons of candied fruit strung on straws and sugared with dust. Here are piles of melons and baskets on baskets of grapes, —these last delicious, it being the sea- son,—and great strings of onions, pyra- mids of tomatoes, and the like. Every- where is a mob in rags apparently intent upon cutting one another's throats to save half a piastre.

Farther on is the Jews' quarter, the street Nischkolitza, with its low houses eked out by awnings under which sit groups of people lounging and talking, and behind these, in little square boxes of rooms let into the wall, squat the money-changers, their bank accounts ex- posed in a small box with a glass top through which can be seen half the coin- age and printage of eastern Europe.

If the king's continued absence caused any uneasiness among the people crowd- ing these streets and bazaars, there was nothing on the surface to indicate it. Many of them looked as if they had very little to lose, and those who had a little more either carried it on their persons in long chains of coins welded

119

together,—a favorite form of safe-de-posit with the Bulgarians,—or, like the money-changers, hived it in a portable box.

Nor could I discover that any one realized that he was living over a powder-magazine with a match-factory next door. On the contrary, everybody was good-natured and happy, chaffing one another across the booths of the bazaars, and bursting into roars of laughter when my brush brought out the features of some well-known street-vender.

The only native who really seemed to possess any positive ideas on the uncer-tain condition of public affairs was a Po-lish Jew, the keeper of the bath, whom I found berating two soldiers for refusing to pay extra for their narghiles, and who expressed to me his contempt for the ruling powers by sweeping in the air a circle which embraced the palace and the offenders, spitting on the floor, and grinding his heel in the moistened spot.

Near the bath, and in fact almost con-nected with it by a rambling row of houses, is one of the few Oriental cafés left in Sofia,—a one-story building with curious sloping roof, its one door open-

ing upon the street corner. It is called the "Maritza." On both sides of this *A Bulgarian Opera Bouffe*
entrance are long, low windows shaped
like those of an old English inn, and beneath these — outside on the sidewalk
— is a row of benches, upon which
lounge idlers sipping coffee and smoking
cigarettes. Within are a motley crew
of all nationalities liberally sprinkled
with Bulgarian soldiers out on a day's
leave.

Coffee is almost the only beverage
in these Turkish cafés. It is always
handed you scalding hot in little, sau-
cerless cups holding hardly a mouthful
each. A glass of cold water invariably
accompanies each cup. This coffee is
generally the finest old Mocha, with an
aroma and flavor unapproachable in any
brand that I know except perhaps the
Uruapam coffee of Mexico. In preparing it the roasted bean is ground as fine
as flour in a hand-mill ; a teaspoonful of
the powder, with half the amount of fine
sugar, being put into a brass pot with a
long handle. To this is added a table-
spoonful of boiling water. The pot is
then thrust into the coals of a charcoal
fire until the coffee reaches boiling point,
when it is caught up by the waiter, who
runs to your table and pours the whole
into your cup. Although it is dark and

121

thick, it is never strong, and there is
not a wakeful hour in a dozen cups.

To me there is nothing so interesting
as one of these Oriental cafés, and so I
turned in from the street, drew a square
straw-covered stool up to a low table,
and held up one finger. A fez-covered
attendant shuffled over and filled my
cup. As I raised it to my lips, my eyes
caught the riveted glance of a black-
bearded man with a beak-like nose and
two ferret eyes watching me intently.
He was dressed in a half-cloak ornamented with a dark braid in twists and
circles, and wore a slouch hat.

Being stared at in a café for the first
five minutes is so usual an experience
for me, in my tramps abroad, that I accept it as part of the conditions of travel.
But there are, of course, different kinds
of stares, all induced and kept up for
the most part by idle curiosity, which
generally ceases after my dress has been
examined, and especially my shoes, and
when my voice has been found to be
like that of other men.

This man's stare, however, was devoid
of curiosity. His was the face of a ferret ; a sly, creeping, half-shrinking face,
with an eye that pierced you one moment and slunk away the next. The
thought flashed through my mind — a

Spanish Jew who hides his gold in a hole, and who is here changing money while the " effervescence " lasts. When I looked agâin a moment later he had disappeared.

The face haunted me so much that I traced its outlines in my sketch-book, trying to remember where I had seen it. I finally persuaded myself that it only suggested some similar face seen long ago. Finishing my coffee, I lighted a cigarette, picked up a stool, and, planting it across the street, began a sketch of the exterior of the café.

The usual crowd gathered, many following me from the room itself, and soon the throng was so great that I could not see the lower lines of the building. No language that I speak is adapted to Bulgaria, and so, rising to my feet, I called out in honest Anglo-Saxon : —

"Get down in front!" This accompanied by a gesture like a policeman's "Move on."

Nobody got down in front, or behind, for that matter. On the contrary, everybody who was down got up, and the sketch was fast becoming hopeless, when four gendarmes arose out of the ground as noiselessly and mysteriously as if they had issued from between the cracks of the paving-stones, formed a hollow

square, with the café at one end and me
at the other, — the intervening space
being as clear of bystanders as the back
of my hand, — and stood like statues
until the sketch was finished. When
I closed my book half an hour later, a
man on the outer edge, wrapped in a
cloak, raised his hand. The crowd fell
back, a gap was made, and the four
gendarmes passed out and were swallowed up.

I turned and caught a glimpse of a
black hat half concealing a dark, bearded
face. It was my friend of the café. Not
a Spanish Jew at all, I said to myself, but
some prominent citizen respected by the
police and anxious to be courteous to
a stranger. And again I dismissed the
face and the incident from my mind.

Just here another face appeared and
another incident occurred, neither of
which was so easily forgotten. The
face enlivened the well-knit, graceful
figure of a young man of thirty dressed
in a gray traveling-suit and wearing a
derby hat. Every line in his good-natured countenance expressed that rarest
and most delightful of combinations, —
humor and grit. From this face proceeded a voice which sent down my
spine that peculiar tingle which one
feels when, half-way across the globe,

surrounded by jargon and heathen, he *A Bulga-* hears suddenly his own tongue, in his *rian Opera Bouffe* own accent, spoken by a fellow-towns-man.

"I heard your 'down in front' and knew right away where you were from ; but these Bashi-bazouks blocked the way. My name is Burton, correspondent of the 'Herald.' Been here two months watching this mouse-trap. Come into the café, where we can talk. You don't know what a godsend an American is in a hole like this."

An interchange of cards settled all formalities, and when, half an hour later, numbers of mutual friends were discovered and inquired after, we grew as confiding and comfortable as if we had been the best of friends through life.

Burton was one of those men of whom everybody hears, whom few people see, and not many people know; one of those men whose homes are fixed by telegrams, whose wits like their pencils are sharpened in emergencies, whose energies are untiring and exhaustless, who ransack, permeate, get at the bottom of things, and endure,— individual men, sagacious, many-sided, and productive, whose whole identity is mercilessly swallowed up and lost in that unnoticed headline, "Our Correspondent."

I had heard of Burton in Paris a few weeks before, where his endless resources in the field and his arctic coolness in tight places were bywords among his fellow-craftsmen. At the time his friends supposed him to be somewhere between Vienna and Constantinople, although none of them located him in Bulgaria ; great morning journals being somewhat reticent as to the identity and whereabouts of their staff.

"Yes," he continued, "life here would reconcile a man to the bottomless pit. I was in London doing some Irish business, — rose in your buttonhole at breakfast, Hyde Park in the afternoon, and all that sort of thing, — when a telegram sent me flying to Paris. Two hours after I was aboard the Orient express, with my shirts half-dried in my bag, and an order in my inside pocket to overhaul Stamboloff and find out whether the prince had left for good, or was waiting until the blow was over before he came back. You see, the Panitza affair came near upsetting things here, and at the time it looked as if the European war circus was about to begin."

"Did you find Stamboloff?" I asked.

"Yes. Reached the frontier, learned he had left Sofia, and, after traveling all

night in a cart, got him at Sistova, and *A Bulga-*
caught our Sunday's edition three hours *rian Opera*
later. Here I have been ever since, *Bouffe*
waiting for something to turn up, and
spending half my nights trying to get
what little does turn up across the frontier and so on to Paris. And the worst
of it is that for four weeks I haven't had
a line from headquarters."

"What! Leave you here in the
lurch?"

"No; certainly not. They write regu-
larly; but these devils stop everything
at the post-office, open and re-seal all
my private letters, and only give me
what they think good for me. For two
weeks past I have been sending my
stuff across the frontier and mailing it
in Servia. How the devil did you get
permission to sketch around here?"

I produced the talismanic scroll with
the water-mark and the image and the
superscription, and related my experience with the prefect.

"Gave you the freedom of the city,
did he? I wager you he will go through
your traps like a custom-house officer
when you leave, and seize everything
you have. They have been doing their
level best to drive me out of here ever
since we published that first interview
with Stamboloff, and they would if they

127

dared. Only, being a correspondent,
you see, and this being a liberal, free
monarchy, it would n't sound well the
next day.

"Come, finish your coffee, and I'll
show you something you can never see
outside of Bulgaria."

We strolled up past the bazaars along
the boulevard, stopping for a moment to
note the cathedral, with one end perched
up in the air, — Stamboloff's commissioners of highways having lowered the
street grade at that point some twenty
feet below the level of the porch floor.

Opposite this edifice was the skylight
of the local photographer. The old, familiar smell of evaporating ether greeted
us as we entered his one-story shop, —
it would be a poetic license to call it a
gallery, — and the usual wooden balcony,
with its painted vase and paper flowers,
grinned at us from its customary place
behind the iron head-rest.

Here were portraits of the prince
and his mother, Princess Clementine,
and of poor Panitza, — whom I really
could not help liking, traitor as he was
to Stamboloff, — and the rest of the
notables, not forgetting the dethroned
prince, Alexander of Battenberg, all of
whom had occupied the plush armchair,
or had stood behind the Venetian railing

128

with the Lake of Como and Mont Blanc in the distance.

Burton hunted through the collection of portraits scattered about the table, and handed me two photographs, — one of a well - built, handsome man with pointed mustache, dressed in the native costume and shackled with heavy chains fastened to his ankles. He was standing in a prison-yard guarded by a soldier holding a carbine.

"Good-looking cut-throat, is n't he? Might be a diplomat or a night editor? Too honest, you think? Well, that's Taco Voyvoda, the famous bandit who was caught a few years ago in the act of murdering a detachment, and who was filled full of lead the next day at the government's expense. Now look at this," and he handed me the other photograph.

I held it to the light, and a shiver ran through me. On a box covered with a piece of canvas rested the head of a man severed from the body. One eye was closed. The other was lost in a ghastly hole, the mark left by a rifle-ball. The mustache was still stiff and pointed, one end drooping a little, and the mouth set firm and determined. The whole face carried an expression as if the death agony had been suddenly frozen into it.

129

About the horror were grouped the bandit's carbine, holsters, and cartridge-belt bristling with cartridges. The belt hung over the matted hair framing the face.

Burton watched me curiously.

"Lovely souvenir, is n't it? The day after the shooting they cut off poor Taco's head, and our friend here" — pointing to the photographer — "fixed him up in this fashion to meet the popular demand. The sale was enormous. Bah! let's go to dinner."

My new-found friend had a better place than the one presided over by my slightly bald waiter with the Tower of Babel education. He would take me to his home. He knew of a garden where a few tables were set, girt about with shrubs and sheltered by overhanging trees that had escaped the drought. At one end was a modest house with a few rooms to let. His gripsack was in one of these. That was why he loved to call it his home.

Soon a white cloth covered a table for two, and a very comfortable dinner was served in the twilight. With the coffee the talk drifted into the present political outlook, and I put the universal conundrum :—

"Will the prince return?"

"You can't tell," said Burton. "For

myself, I believe he will. He must do
so if he wants to see his money again,
and he can do so in safety if Stamboloff
succeeds in carrying the elections next
month, which I believe he will. If he
fails, the nearer they all hug the frontier
the better; for there are hundreds of
men right here around us who would
serve every one of them as the soldiers
did Taco Voyvoda. They know it, too,
for they are all off electioneering except
the prince, who, I understand, has left
Ryllo to-day for Varna. He is hanging
on the telegraph now. Not the poles,
but the dispatches.

"The worst feature of the situation
is that most of the factions are backed
up by Russian and other agents, each in
their several interests, ready to lend a
hand. To-day it is a game of chess between Russia and Turkey; to-morrow it
may involve all Europe. Through it all
my sympathies are with the prince. He
has been here now nearly three years
trying to make something of these bar-
barians, and so far not a single European power has recognized him. He
will get nothing for his pains, poor fellow. When his money is all gone they
will bounce him as they did Battenberg.

"Certain members of the cabinet are
not safe even now," continued Burton.

131

"While I was at Sistova, the other day, I had an opportunity of seeing some of the risks that Stamboloff himself runs, and also how carefully he is guarded. He was in a café taking his breakfast. As soon as he entered, a tall sergeant of gendarmes with his sabre half-drawn and his red sash stuck full of pistols and yataghans moved to his right side, while another equally ferocious and as heavily armed guarded his left. Then the doors were blocked by half a dozen other gendarmes, who watched everybody's movements. There is really not so much solid fun being prime minister in Bulgaria as one would think."

While Burton was speaking three officers entered the garden where we were dining and took possession of an adjoining table. My friend nodded to one of them and kept on talking, lowering his voice a trifle and moving his chair so that his face could not be seen.

The Bulgarians were in white uniforms and carried their side-arms.

The next instant a young man entered hurriedly, looked about anxiously, and came straight towards our table. When he caught sight of me he drew back. Burton motioned him to advance, and turned his right ear for a long whispered communication, interrupting him occasionally by such telephone exclamations as, "Who told you so? When? How did he find out? To-morrow? What infernal nonsense! I don't believe a word of it," etc.

The young man bent still lower, looked furtively at the officers, and in an inaudible whisper poured another message into Burton's ear.

My host gave a little start and turned a trifle pale.

"The devil, you say! Better come to my room, then, to-night at twelve."

"Anything up?" I asked after the man had gone, noticing the change in Burton's manner.

"Well, yes. My assistant tells me that my last letter has been overhauled this side of the frontier, and that orders for my arrest will be signed to-morrow. I don't believe it. But you can't tell, — these people are fools enough to do any-thing. If I knew which of my letters had reached our office I would n't care; but I have n't seen our paper since my first dispatches appeared, more than a month ago."

"That need n't worry you. I have every one of them in my bag at the ho-tel, and every issue of your paper since you arrived here. I knew I was coming, and I wanted to be posted."

Burton looked at me in open astonish-ment.

"You!"

"Certainly. Come to my room; get them in five minutes."

"Well, that paralyzes me! Here I have been stranded for news and blocked for weeks by these brigands who rob my mail, and here you pick me up in the streets and haul everything I want out of your carpet-bag! Don't ever put that in a story, for nobody would ever be-lieve it. Give me a cigarette."

I opened my case, and as I handed him its contents my eyes rested on a man watching us intently. He was sit-ting at the officers' table. With the flar-ing of Burton's match his face came into full relief.

It was my friend of the morning.

"There he is again," I blurted out.

"Who?" said Burton without mov-ing.

"The man in the Turkish café, — the one who ordered the soldiers around. Who is he?"

Burton never moved a muscle of his face except to blow rings over his coffee-cup.

"A mean-looking hound in a slouch hat, with rat-terrier eyes, bushy beard, and a bad-fitting cloak?"

"Yes," said I, comparing the description over his shoulder.

"Why! that's my shadow, — a delicate
attention bestowed on me by the prefect.
He thinks I don't know him, but I fool
him every day. I got two columns out
last night from under his very nose, —
right at this table. The waiter carried
them off in a napkin, and my man
nabbed them outside."

"A spy?"

"No ; a shadow, a night-hawk. For
nearly two months this fellow has never
taken his eyes off me, and yet he has
never seen me look him in the face.
Come, these people are getting too so-
ciable."

In an instant we were in the street,
and in three minutes had entered my
hotel. Leaving Burton in the hall, I
mounted the broad staircase, went
straight to my room, picked up my
pocket sketch-book, and thrust the
"clippings" into my inside pocket.

When I regained the corridor outside
my door the man in the slouch hat preceded me downstairs!

Smothering my astonishment, — I had
left him sitting in the garden five minutes before, — I followed slowly, match-
ing my steps to his, and turning over in
my mind whether it would be best to

135

swallow the clippings or drop them over
the balusters.

I could see Burton below, standing
near the door absorbed in an Orient express time-table tacked to the wall. (I
was to leave for Constantinople the next
day.) He must have heard our footsteps,
but he never turned his head.

The man reached the hall floor, — I
was five steps behind, — stood within
ten feet of Burton, and began striking
matches for a cigar which was still burn-
ing.

I decided instantly.

"Oh ! Burton," I called out, " I found
the sketch-book. See what I did here
yesterday ; " and I ran rapidly over the
leaves, noting as I turned, "The Jews'
Quarter" — "Minaret of Bania-bashie"
— "Ox-Team down by the Bazaar," etc.

The man lingered, and I could feel
him looking over my shoulder. Then
the glass door clicked, and he disappeared.

Burton raised his hand warningly.

"Where did you pick *him* up ? "

"Outside my door."

"Keyhole business, eh ? Did you get
them ? "

I touched my inside pocket.

"Good." And he slipped the pack-
age of clippings under his waistcoat.

136

The next morning I found this note *A Bulgarian Opera Bouffe* tucked under my door : —

"The game is up. Meet me at station at twelve.   BURTON."

Five minutes before the appointed hour my traps were heaped up in one corner of the waiting-room.

I confess to a certain degree of anxiety as I waited in the station, both on my own account and on his. I was unable to understand how the night-hawk could have reached my chamber door ahead of me unless he had sailed over the roof and dropped down the chimney, and I was equally willing to admit that something besides a desire to see me safely in bed had induced him to keyhole my movements. Perhaps his sudden disappearance through the glass door was, after all, only preparatory to including me in the attentions he was reserving for Burton.

When the exact hour arrived, and the Orient express direct for Philippopolis and Constantinople rolled into the depot, and still Burton did not appear, I began to realize the absurdity of waiting for a convict at the main entrance. Bur-

137

ton of course would be chained to two soldiers and placed in a baggage-van, or perhaps be shackled around the ankles like Voyvoda and lifted out of a cart by his waistband. The yard was the place to find him.

I made my way between the two door-guards, who eyed me in a manner that convinced me that I was under surveillance and would most likely catch both balls in the vicinity of my collar-button if I attempted to move out of range.

But there was nothing in the yard except empty cars and a squad of raw recruits sitting on their bundles awaiting transportation, and so I tried the boulevard side again.

No Burton.

Just as I was about to give him up for lost and had begun turning over in my mind what my duty might be as a man and an American, a fresh cloud of dust blew in the open door, and a cab pulled up. From this emerged a pair of leather gaiters followed by two legs in check trousers, a hand with white wristbands and English gloves, and last the cool, unruffled face of Burton himself.

"Yes, I am late, but I have been up all night dictating. You got my note, I see. I go as far with you as Philippopo-

138

lis, where I get out to reach the Pomuk
Highlands. You remember I told you
about that old brigand chief, Achmet
Aga, who rules a province of forty
square miles and pays tribute to no one,
not even the Sultan. You know he
murders everybody who crosses his line
without his permission. Well, I am
going to interview him."

This was said in one breath and with
as much ease of manner and indifference
to surroundings as if the man with a
slouch hat had been an idle dream instead of an active reality.

"But what about your arrest, Burton?
I expected " —

"Expected what — dungeons? Nonsense. I simply went out on my balcony
last night before I crawled into bed,
sneezed, and called out in French to my
man inside to pack my bag for this
train. That satisfied my shadow, for all
he wants is to get me out of the way.
Don't worry; the dog will be here to
see us off."

Burton was right. That ugly face was
the last that peered at us as we rolled
out of the station.

Six hours later I left my new friend
at Philippopolis with a regret I cannot
explain, but with an exacted promise to
meet me in Constantinople a week

139

later, where we would enjoy the Turks together.

The week passed, and another, and then a third, and still no sign of Burton. I had begun to wonder whether, after all, the brigand chief had not served him as he had done his predecessors, when this letter, dated Sofia, reached me : —

"Just returned from the mountains. Spent a most delightful week with Achmet Aga, who kissed me on both cheeks when I left, and gave me a charm against fire and sword blessed by all the wise women of the clan. Would have joined you before, but had to hurry back here for the opening of the Sobranje.

"Stamboloff's party carried the day by a small majority, and the town is full of his men, including the prince, who opened parliament here yesterday."

VII. CAPTAIN JOE

ANTED — A submarine engineer, experienced in handling heavy stone under water. Apply, etc.

In answer to this advertisement, a man wearing a rough jacket and looking like a sailor opened my office door.

" I'm Captain Joe Bell, out of a job. Seein' your advertisement, I called up. Where is the work, and what is it?"

I explained briefly. A lighthouse was to be built in the " Race," off Fisher's Island, — the foundation of rough stone protected by granite blocks weighing ten tons each. These blocks were to be laid by a diver, as an enrockment, their edges touching. The current in the Race ran six miles an hour. This increased the difficulties of the work.

While my visitor bent over the plans, tracing each detail with a blunted finger that looked like a worn-out thole-pin, I had time to look him over. He was about fifty years of age, powerfully built, short, and as broad as he was long. The very fit of his clothes indicated his

enormous strength. His pea-jacket had
long since been pulled out of shape in
the effort to accommodate itself to the
spread of his shoulders. His trousers
were corrugated, and half-way up his
ankles, in the perpetual struggle to protect equally seat and knee, — each wrin-
kle outlining a knotted muscle, twisted
up and down a pair of legs short and
sturdy as rudder-posts. His brown hair
protruded from under a close-fitting cloth
cap, and curled over a neck seamed and
bronzed, showing bumps where almost
every other man had hollows: these
short curls were streaked with gray.
His face was round, ruddy, and wind-
tanned, the chin hidden in a stubby
beard, which clung to his lower lip; the
mouth was firm, the teeth a row of corn,
the jaws strong and determined. Everything about him indicated reserve force,
endurance, capacity, and push.

Two things struck me instantly: a
voice which was rich and musical, and
an eye which looked through me, — a
clear, laughing, kindling, tender eye,
that changed every instant, boring like
a gimlet as he pored over the plans, or
lighting up with a flash in the sugges-
tion of ways and means to carry them
out.

As he leaned over the table, I noticed

that his wrist was bandaged, the cotton wrappings showing beneath his coat-sleeve, discovering a partly healed scar.

"Burnt?" I asked.

"No, scraped. It don't bother now, but it was pretty bad a month back."

"How?"

"Oh, a-wreckin'. I've been four years with the Off-Shore Wreckin' Company. Left yesterday."

"What for?"

He looked straight at me, and said, slowly emphasizing each word :—

"Me and the president did n't gee. He had n't no fault to find with me ; but I did n't like his ways, and I quit."

So transparent was his honesty, self-reliance, and grit that such precautionary measures as references or inquiries never once entered my mind. Before he left my room the terms were agreed upon. The following week he took charge of the force, and the work began.

As the summer passed away the masses of granite were lowered into position, Captain Joe placing each block himself, the steam-lighter holding to her anchors in the rip of the Race.

When the autumn came a cottage was rented on the shore of the nearest harbor, and the captain's family of six

143

moved in. Later I noticed two new faces in the home circle :— a pale, sad woman and a delicate-looking child, both dressed in black. They would sometimes remain a week, and then disappear only to return again. The mother was introduced by the captain as " Jennie, widow of my old mate Jim."

"What happened to him, Captain Joe ? " I asked one evening, when she left the room to take the child to bed. He was sitting near the window, from which could be caught a glimpse in the twilight of the tall masts of the schooners, coal-laden, and the jibs of the smacks at anchor near the village wharves.

"Drownded, sir ; two year ago." And he looked the other way.

"Washed overboard ? " I asked, noticing his husky voice.

" No. Smothered in his divin'-dress, with a dumb fool at the other end of his life-line. We wuz to work on the Scotland, sunk in six fathoms of water off Sandy Hook. The president sent for me to come to the city, and I left Jim alone. That week we wuz workin' in her lower hold, Jim and me, I tendin' and Jim divin', and then I goin' below and he lookin' out after my air hose and line. Me bein' away that day, they

144

put a duffer at the pump. Jim got his
hose tangled up in a fluke of the anchor ;
they misunderstood his signals, and
hauled taut when they should have
eased away. ‸ He made a dash at the
hose with his knife, but whether it wuz
the brass wire wove in it, or because he
wuz beat for breath, we don't know.
Anyways he warn't strong enough to
cut her through, and when they got him
up he wuz done for. That wuz mighty
rough on me, bein' with Jim mor'n ten
years, in and out o' water. So I look
out for Jennie and the young one. No,
it ain't nothin' strange nor new. While
I've got a roof over me she's welcome.
He'd done the same for me, and I've
got the best of it, for there's only two of
his'n, and there's six o' mine."

As the work on the lighthouse pro-
gressed the force and plant increased.
A steam-tug was added, stone-sloops
were chartered, and the gradual filling
up of the interior of the foundation began.

The owner of one of these sloops was
a tall, sunken-cheeked old man named
Marrows, who lived near the village on
a small stone-incrusted farm. Outside
of its scanty crop this vessel and her
earnings were his sole resource.

Late one afternoon his sloop returned

145

to the harbor with her shrouds loose, her mast started, and her forefoot chewed into splinters. It seemed that her captain, a retired, bony fisherman, named Barrett, had miscalculated the tide, which cut like a mill-tail in the Race. She had misstayed and swirled, bow on, atop of the enrockment of the lighthouse. When she struck, Captain Joe was in his diving dress, his helmet off. In a moment he had loosed his heavy iron shoes, caught up a crowbar, and was bounding over the rugged rocks surrounding the foundation, giving quick, sharp orders to his men, who sprang into a yawl and began paying out a heavy line.

The next instant he was under the sloop's bowsprit, his broad back braced against her chains, his legs rigid as hydraulic jacks. Every time the vessel surged he straightened out, concentrating his enormous strength and assisting the backward movement, so that when she lunged again she came a few inches short of the jagged rocks, the wave having spent its force. There he stood for half an hour, shaking his head free from the great sheets of white foam breaking clear over him, shouting his orders between the sousings of the waves, until the men in the yawl had slung a kedge

146

anchor away out astern of the endan- gered sloop, and she was windlassed clear of the stone pile and saved.

Marrows was on the little dock, peering through the twilight, when his rescued sloop returned to the village harbor. Captain Joe held the tiller. He began as soon as Marrows's gaunt figure, outlined against the evening sky, caught his eye : —

"I tell you, old man, Captain Barrett ain't fittin' to fool round that rock. He 'll get hurt. I tell you he ain't fittin'."

"I believe you, and I 've told him so. Is she sprung, Captain Joe ? "

"A leetle mite forrard, and her mast a touch to starboard, but nothin' to hurt."

"Will she be any good any more ? " Then, as he came nearer, "Why, you 're soaking wet : the boys say you was clear under her." Then, lowering his voice, "You know, Captain Joe, she is a good deal to me."

The captain laid his great rough hand tenderly on the old man's shoulder.

"I know it, I know it; that 's why I wuz under her chains." Then, raising his voice, "But Barrett ain't fittin'; mind I tell you he ain't fittin'."

The next day being stormy, with a

gale outside and no work possible, Captain Joe tightened up the shrouds of the disabled sloop himself, reset the mast, lecturing Barrett all the while, and then sent word to Marrows that she was "tight as a keg, better 'n ever, and everythin' aboard, 'ceptin' the bony fisherman, who was out of a job."

The winter closed in with the foundation but partly completed. Before the first December gale broke on the rock the derricks were stripped of their rigging and left to battle with the winter's storms, the tools were stowed in the shanty, and all work suspended until the spring. During the long winter that followed Captain Joe took to the sea, having transferred his diving-gear to the sloop; and before April three coal-laden schooners were anchored, or stranded, as befitted their condition, on the shoals in front of his dock in the village harbor. It made no difference to him how severe was the gale, or how badly strained the helpless vessel, he was under her bottom almost as soon as a line could reach her. Then a patch of canvas, or half a cargo of empty oil-barrels, buoyed her up until the tug could tighten a line over her bow, and tow her to an anchorage inside the lighthouse.

148

It seemed in truth that winter as if each luckless craft, in its journey up the Sound, did its level best to keep its rail above water long enough to sink peacefully and restfully upon some bar or shoal within reach of Captain Joe's diving-tackle. There it died contented, feeling sure of a speedy resurrection.

If a wrecked schooner, coal-laden, was an unusual sight along the harbor shore, a wrecker distributing her cargo free to his neighbors was a proceeding unknown to the oldest inhabitant. And yet this always occurred when a fresh wreck grounded on the flats.

"That's all right," he would say; "better take a couple of boat-loads more. Seems to me as if we wuz goin' to have a late spring. No, I don't know the price, 'cause I ain't settled with the underwriters; but then she came up mighty easy for me, and a few tons don't make no difference, nohow."

When the settling day came, and his share as salvage was determined upon, there was of course a heavy shortage. He always laughed heartily.

"Better put that down to me," he would say to the agent. "Some of the folks along here boated off a little. Guess they wuz careless, and did n't know how much they took."

149

Little indiscretions like this soon endeared him to his neighbors. Before long every one up and down the shore knew him, and everybody sent a cheery word flying after him whenever they caught sight of his active, restless figure moving along the vessel's deck, or busy about his dock and wrecking-gear. Even the gruff doctor would crane his head around the edge of his curtained wagon to call out "Good-morning," although he might be clear out of hailing distance.

So passed the winter.

When the first breath of spring blew over the marsh the shanty for the men on the rock was rebuilt and the work resumed.

During all these months the captain never once referred to his early life or associations, or gave me the slightest clue to his antecedents. Now and then he would speak of Jim, his dead mate, as being a "cur'us square man," and occasionally he would refer to the president of the Off-shore Wrecking Company, his former employer, as "that skin." Such information as I did gather about his earlier days was fragmentary and disconnected, and generally came from his men, who idolized him, and who had absolute belief in his judgment and the blindest confidence in his cease-

150

less care for their personal safety. This
care was necessary : the swiftness of the
current and sudden changes of wind,
bringing in a heavy southeast roll, sub-
merging the rock at wave intervals,
while the slippery, slimy surface and the
frequent falling of the heavy derricks
made the work extremely dangerous.
He deserved their confidence, for
through his constant watchfulness but
one man was hurt on the work during
the six years of its construction, and this
occurred during the captain's absence.

One morning when tacking across the
Race in a small boat in a stiff breeze,
with only the captain and myself for
crew, I tried to make him talk of himself
and his earlier life, and so said, suddenly :

"Oh, Captain Joe ! I met a friend of
yours yesterday who wished me to ask
you how you stopped the leak in the
Hoboken ferry-boat, and why you left
the employ of the Off-shore Wrecking
Company."

He raised his eyes quickly, a smile
lighting his weather-beaten face.

"Who was it — the president ? " He
always spoke of his former employer in
that way.

" Yes, — but of one of the big insur-
ance companies ; not your Wrecking
Company."

"No, reck'n not. He ought to keep pretty still about it."

"Tell me about it."

"Oh, there ain't nothin' to tell. She got foul of a tug, and listed some, and I sorter plugged her up till they hauled her into the slip. Been so long ago I 'most forgot about it."

But not another word could be coaxed out of him, except that he remembered that the water was "blamed cold," and his arm was "pretty well tore up for a month."

That night, in the shanty which was built on the completed part of the work, and which sheltered the working force for the three years of this section of the construction, were gathered a crew of a dozen men, many of whom had served with Captain Joe when Jim was alive. While the captain was asleep in the little wooden bunk, boarded off for his especial use, the ceaseless thrash of the sea sounding in our ears, I managed, after much questioning and piecing out of personal reminiscences, to gather these details.

One morning in January, two years before, when the ice in the Hudson River ran unusually heavy, a Hoboken ferry-boat slowly crunched her way through the floating floes, until the

thickness of the pack choked her pad-
dles in mid-river. The weather had
been bitterly cold for weeks, and the
keen northwest wind had blown the
great fields of floating ice into a hard
pack along the New York shore. It
was the early morning trip, and the
decks were crowded with laboring men,
and the driveways choked with teams;
the women and children standing inside
the cabins, a solid mass up to the swinging doors. While she was gathering
strength for a further effort, an ocean
tug sheered to avoid her, veered a point,
and crashed into her side, cutting her
below the water-line in a great V-shaped
gash. The next instant a shriek went
up from a hundred throats. Women,
with blanched faces, caught terror-
stricken children in their arms, while
men, crazed with fear, scaled the rails
and upper decks to escape the plunging
of the overthrown horses. The disabled boat careened from the shock
and fell over on her beam helpless.
Into the V-shaped gash the water poured
a torrent. It seemed but a question of
minutes before she would lunge headlong below the ice.

Within two hundred yards of both
boats, and free of the heaviest ice,
steamed the wrecking tug Reliance of

153

the Off-shore Wrecking Company, making her way cautiously up the New Jersey shore to coal at Weehawken. On her deck forward, sighting the heavy cakes, and calling out cautionary orders to the mate in the pilot-house, stood Captain Joe. When the ocean tug reversed her engines after the collision and backed clear of the shattered wheel-house of the ferry-boat, he sprang forward, stooped down, ran his eye along the water-line, noted in a flash every shattered plank, climbed into the pilot-house of his own boat, spun her wheel hard down, and before the astonished pilot could catch his breath ran the nose of the Reliance along the rail of the ferry-boat and dropped upon the latter's deck like a cat.

If he had fallen from a passing cloud the effect could not have been more startling. Men crowded about him and caught at his hands. Women sank on their knees, and hugged their children, and a sudden peace and stillness possessed every soul on board. Tearing a life-preserver from the man nearest him and throwing it overboard, he backed the coward ahead of him through the swaying mob, ordering the people to stand clear, and forcing the whole mass to the starboard side. The increased

154

weight gradually righted the stricken boat until she regained a nearly even keel.

With a threat to throw overboard any man who stirred, he dropped into the engine-room, met the engineer half-way up the ladder, compelled him to return, dragged the mattresses from the crew's bunks, stripped off blankets, racks of clothes, overalls, cotton waste, and rags of carpet, cramming them into the great rent left by the tug's cutwater, until the space of each broken plank was replaced, except one. Through and over this space the water still combed, deluging the floors and swashing down between the gratings into the hold below.

"Another mattress, quick! All gone? A blanket, then — carpet — anything — five minutes more and she'll right herself. Quick, for God's sake!"

It was useless. Everything, even to the oil-rags, had been used.

"Your coat, then. Think of the babies, man; do you hear them?"

Coats and vests were off in an instant; the engineer on his knees bracing the shattered planking, Captain Joe forcing the garments into the splintered openings.

It was useless. Little by little the water gained, bursting out first below, then on one side, only to be recaulked, and only to rush in again.

Captain Joe stood a moment as if undecided, ran. his eye searchingly over the engine-room, saw that for his needs it was empty, then deliberately tore down the top wall of caulking he had so carefully built up, and, before the engineer could protest, had forced his own body into the gap with his arm outside level with the drifting ice.

An hour later the disabled ferry-boat, with every soul on board, was towed into the Hoboken slip.

When they lifted him from the wreck he was unconscious and barely alive. The water had frozen his blood, and the floating ice had torn the flesh from his protruding arm, from shoulder to wrist. When the color began to creep back to his cheeks, he opened his eyes, and said to the doctor who was winding the bandages : —

" Wuz any of them babies hurt ? "

A month passed before he regained his strength, and another week before the arm had healed so that he could get his coat on. Then he went back to his work on board the Reliance.

In the mean time the Off-shore Wrecking Company had presented a bill to the ferry company for salvage, claiming that the safety of the ferry-boat was due to one of the employees of the Wrecking Company. Payment had been refused, resulting in legal proceedings, which had already begun. The morning following this action Captain Joe was called into the president's office.

"Captain," said that official, "we're going to have some trouble getting our pay for that ferry job. Here's an affidavit for you to swear to."

The captain took the paper to the window and read it through without a comment, then laid it back on the president's desk, picked up his hat, and moved to the door.

"Did you sign it?"

"No; and I ain't a-goin' to."

"Why?"

"'Cause I ain't so durned mean as you be. Look at this arm. Do you think I'd got into that hell-hole if it had n't 'a' been for them women cryin' and the babies a-hollerin'? And you want 'em to pay for it. If your head wuz n't white, I'd mash it."

Then he walked straight to the cashier, demanded his week's pay, waited until the money was counted out, slammed the office door behind him, and walked

157

out, cursing like a pirate. The next day he answered my advertisement.

The following year, when the masonry was rapidly nearing the top or coping course, and the five years of labor were bringing forth their fruit, the foundation and the pier being then almost ready for the keeper's house and lantern, — its light has flashed a welcome to many a storm-driven coaster ever since, — I was sitting one lovely spring morning overlooking the sea, the rock with its cluster of derricks being just visible far out on the water-line.

Beside me sat a man famous in the literature of our country, — one who had embalmed in song and story the heroic deeds of common men, which are now, and will be, household words as long as the language is read. To him I outlined the story, adding : —

"It is but half a mile to the captain's cottage, and, being Sunday morning, we shall find him at home ; let him tell it in his own way."

We took the broad road skirting the shore, overlooking the harbor with its white yachts glinting against the blue. High up, reveling in the warm sunlight, the gray gulls poised and curved, while across the yellow marshes the tall tower of the harbor light was penciled against the morning sky. Over old fences, patched with driftwood and broken oars and festooned with fishermen's nets, stretched the boughs of apple-trees loaded with blossoms, and in scattered sheltered spots the buttercups and dandelions brightened the green grass. A turn in the road, a swinging gate, a flagged path leading to the porch of a low cottage, and a big burly fellow held out both hands. It was Captain Joe. He was in his Sunday best, with white shirt-sleeves, his face clean-shaven to the very edge of the tuft on his chin.

With a child on each knee, the younger a new-comer since the building of the lighthouse, he talked of the "work," his neighbors, the "wrack" the winter before, — the one on Fisher's Island, when the captain was drowned, — the late spring, the cussed sou'east wind that kep' a-blowin' till you thought it were n't never goin' to wollup round to the west'ard again ; in short, of everything — but himself.

My beating the bush with allusions to sinking vessels, collisions at sea, suits for salvage, and the like only flushed up such reminiscences as fall to the lot of

159

seafaring men the world over — but no-thing more. In despair I put the question straight at him.

"Tell him, Captain Joe, of that morning in the ice off Hoboken, when you boarded the ferry-boat."

He would, but he had 'most forgot, been so long ago. So many of these things a-comin' up when a man's bangin' round, it's hard to keep track on 'em. Remembered there wuz a mess of people aboard, mostly women and babies, and they wuz all a-hollerin' to wunst. He wuz workin' on the Reliance at the time, — captain of her. Come to think of it, he found her log last week in his old sea-chest, when he wuz lookin' for some rubber cloth to patch his divin'-suit. If his wife would get the book out, he guessed it wuz all there. He wuz always partic'ler about keepin' log aboard ship.

When the old well-thumbed book was found, he perched his glasses on his nose, and began turning the leaves with that same old thole-pin of a finger, stopping at every page to remoisten it, and adding a running commentary of his own over the long-forgotten records.

"*January 23.* — Yes! that's when we worked on the Hurricane. She was sunk off Sandy Hook, loaded with su-

gar; nasty mess that. It was somewhere about that time, for I remember
the water wuz pretty cold, and the ice
a-runnin'. Ah! here it is. Knowed I
had n't forgot it. You can read it
yourself; my eyes ain't so good as they
wuz" — pointing to the entry on the
ink-stained page.

It read as follows : —

" *January 30.* — Left Jersey City 7
A. M. Ice running heavy. Captain
Joe stopped leak in ferry-boat."

VIII. HUTCHINS

UTCHINS lived at the foot of the hill, in a battered, patched-up shanty of broken windows and half-hinged doors. The neighbors told queer stories about this rookery, and when they could passed by on the other side. Time had stained its unpainted boards a dull gray. Untidy women hung about the porch crowded with wash-tubs, while cooking utensils, broken pots, and fragments of a rusty summer stove littered the steps and out-house roof.

The only spot that defied the filth and squalor was a little patch of a garden shut in by a broken fence. This held a dozen rows of corn, a stray stalk of morning-glory clinging to a bent and tottering pole, a flaming stand of hollyhock, and a few overgrown sprouts of turnip rioting in the freedom of their neglect.

Hutchins himself, except at rare intervals, always leaned lazily in the propped-up doorway, a ragged, dirt-begrimed tramp, biting savagely at the

end of a clay pipe. Besotted, blear-
eyed and vulgar, with thin, loosely jointed
legs and bent shoulders, he looked his
reputation, — the terror of the neighbor-
hood.

Nobody tried to understand the family. The nearest neighbors, generally
reliable in such cases, could give no
clear description of its members, for
they never entered his door. They all
agreed, however, upon one fact, — that
the tall girl who worked in the factory,
and who had come home three years before to nurse another baby, — this time
her own, — was Hutchins' only daughter.

Outside this battered wreck of a home,
with its frowzy inmates, Hutchins' only
possessions were a pair of lean, half-fed
oxen who gained a scanty living by nib-
bling at the patches of grass which grew
along the county road. Now and then
in the haying season, or when the heavy
timber was hauled to the mill, or the
road commissioners repaired the highway, their owner would yoke them to a
sun-bleached, unpainted cart as shaky
as himself. This combination in the
twilight, when his day's work was done,
made a gruesome picture, as it stum-
bled down the steep wood road that led
by one side of my house, on the way
163

to his own.   He never walked by the head of his oxen, as did most country-men, but always propped himself up in his cart, his slouching, swaying figure outlined against the sky, his thin legs hanging below the tailboard.   When the children, guessing his condition, — the hire of the cart was always left in the tavern at the fork of the road, — called jeeringly at him, he would slide off the board and begin to throw stones. When my dog ran out, he would coax him near and then lash him with his whip.   These idiosyncrasies did not endear him to his neighbors.

I have always had a sympathy for the man who is down, and so, when I met Hutchins I always said "Good-morn-ing" as pleasantly as I could.   I never remember having said much else, nor that he ever made any other reply than a nod of his head or a short "Mornin'" hissed out between his teeth, as if the effort hurt him.

The road to my work ran by Hutchins' gate, and there, one morning, for the first time, I saw the little golden-haired grandchild who had furnished the win-ter nights' gossip for three years past.

When this day I stopped and spoke to the child, Hutchins slouched out from his door, called to her mother, and when

the child cried and started towards me, *Hutchins*
caught up a stick angrily. Something
in her face, or perhaps mine, stopped
him, for when she lifted up her dimpled
fingers and ran towards me he softened
and walked sullenly away.

Little by little the child and I became
fast friends. She would toddle out to
watch for me when I passed by in the
morning, her hair flying in the wind.
Sometimes, too, she would thrust her
chubby sunburned hand through the
broken palings and toss out a gay-colored
hollyhock that blossomed low enough
on its stalk for her to reach.

As the friendship grew it ripened
into an intimacy that finally culminated
in her walking with me one day as
far as the little bridge over the brook.
These confidential relations seemed to
impart their flavor to the rest of the
family. I noticed that my little friend
seemed less untidy, and one morning
her outcast of a mother, hearing my
voice, put a clean apron over her own
head, thus recognizing the unkempt
condition of her hair. As for Hutchins, although he never offered to speak
first, he would somehow manage to have
his hat in his hand when I approached,
— his best attempt at a courtesy. If,
however, he held me in any different
165

esteem from the rest of his neighbors, or rather if he hated me the less, there was nothing in his manner to show it, except the slight evidences I have indicated.

When I lost my setter dog, search was made in the village, and up and down the highway as far as the stage went. The farmers, of course, accused Hutchins. Everything from the robbing of a hen-roost to the big burglary of the county bank was laid at his door. At first I was a little suspicious, and to test his knowledge of my loss offered a reward. A week later I found the dog tied to my door, and the next day learned from my foreman that the poor fellow had followed a gunner, and that Hutchins, hearing of it, had walked twelve miles to the next village to bring him back. When I taxed him with it he made no answer, and when I handed him the reward he dropped the banknote on the ground and lounged off whistling.

Winter came, and my work was still unfinished. Affairs at Hutchins' were unchanged. The house perhaps looked a little more tumbled-down, — the gable ends, porch, and sloping roof hugging the big chimney the closer, as if they feared the coming cold. The neigh-

bors still avoided the place, the women
pretending not to see the daughter when
she passed, and the men leering at her
when they dared.

As for the daughter, my acquaintance
with her had never extended beyond
a word now and then about the child,
which was always answered in a half-
frightened, shrinking way.

One blustering night — it was the last
week in December — I was sitting in
my room alone studying some plans
of a coffer-dam for the better protec-
tion of a submarine foundation I was
building, when there came a sharp
knock at the outer door. I expected
one of my men, and, catching up the
lamp, shot back the bolt and raised the
light aloft. A gust of snow chilled my
face, nearly extinguishing the flame.
Outside the snow lay in drifts, the
lower branches of the cedars being half
buried, while the stretch to the lower
gate was an unbroken sheet of white.
Around the corner of the porch my
eyes caught the marks of a straggling,
uneven footstep ; and beyond, hurrying
over the lower fence, I could barely
distinguish the outline of a shrunken,
shambling figure. It was Hutchins.

Stooping over to bring in the mat,
now wet with snow, my mind filled with
167

the strange visit and the stranger hurried disappearance, my hand touched a bundle tied with a cotton cord. It had evidently been laid there but a moment before. It was hard and round and wrapped in a newspaper.

I brought it to my fire and cut the string. Inside was a huge turnip the size of my two fists ; fastened to it was a sprig of holly. I looked up, and my eye fell on the calendar upon my mantel.

It was Christmas Eve.

IX. SIX HOURS IN SQUAN-TICO

QUANTICO was not my destination.

I confess to hearing from my berth in the Pullman, when the train stopped in the depot, all the customary sounds, — the bumpings and couplings of the cars, the relieved " whuff ! " of the locomotive catching its breath after the night's run, the shouts of the hackmen, and the rumbling of the baggage trucks. I remember also the " Dust you off, sir," of the suddenly attentive porter levying blackmail with his brush, the glare of the lanterns, and blinding flash of the head-light. All this came to me as I lay half awake in my section, but — it did not suggest Squantico.

On the contrary, it meant prospective peace and comfort, and another hour's nap, when I would finally be side-tracked outside the station in Washington. So I turned over and enjoyed it.

Experience teaches me that the going astray of the best laid plans is not con-

169

fined wholly to men and mice; it includes Pullmans.

My first intimation of disaster came from the expectant blackmailer.

"Eight o'clock, sir; last berth occupied."

More positive data proceeded from the conductor, who clicked a punch under my nose and blurted out, "Tickets!"

I fumbled mechanically under my pillow, and, remembering, said sleepily, "Gave them to you last night."

"Not to me. Want your tickets for Richmond."

I sat up. Whole rows of people dressed for the day were quietly and contentedly occupying their seats. All the berths had been swept away. My curtains alone dangled from the continuous brass rod. Every eye in the car was fastened on my traveling bedroom.

"I am not going to Richmond. I get off at Washington."

"Wrong car, sir. Left Washington two hours ago."

"Stop at the next station," I gasped, grabbing my coat.

The conductor peered through the car window, pulled the bell-rope, and shouted, "All out for Squantico!" The next moment I was shivering in a pool of snow and water, my bag bottom side up, the rear of the retreating train filling Six Hours in Squantico a distant cut.

A man in a fur hat and blue overcoat cast his eye my way, picked up a mail-pouch from a half-melted snow-bank, and preceded me up a muddy road flanked by a worm-fence. I overtook him, and added my bag to his load.

"When can I get back to Washington?"

"Ten minutes past two."

I made a hurried calculation. Six hours! Six hours in a hole like this!

It was not a cheery morning for landing anywhere. January-thaw mornings never are. A drizzling rain saturated everything. A steaming fog hung over the low country, drifted out over the river, and made ghosts of the piles of an unfinished dock. The mud was inches deep under the snow, which lay sprawling out in patches, covering the ground like a worn-out coat. A dozen cheaply constructed houses and stores built of wood fronted on one side of a broad road. Opposite the group was a great barn of a building, with its doors and lower windows boarded up. This was the hotel.

Before I had turned the road I had learned all that could possibly interest me : the hotel was closed; Colonel Jar-

171

vis kept a store third house from the corner; and Mrs. Jarvis could get me a breakfast.

The man with the pouch exchanged my bag for a dime, pointed to a collection of empty dry-goods boxes ranged along the sidewalk ahead, and disappeared within a door bearing a swinging tin sign marked "Post-Office." I rounded the largest box, climbed the steps, and entered the typical country store.

" Is Colonel Jarvis in ? "

Four men hugging a cast-iron stove pushed back their chairs. One — a lank, chin-bearded Virginian — straightened himself out and came forward. He wore a black slouch hat, a low-cut velvet vest with glass buttons,— all gone but two, — a shoestring necktie, and a pair of carpet slippers very much run down at the heel. The only redeeming points about him were his voice, which though clogged with the richest of Virginia dialects was still soft and flexible, and his manners, in which were visible some slight outcroppings of a gentility buried with the preceding generation. Regarded from the point of view of a traveler half awake, hungry, wet, and wholly disgusted, his appearance only helped to intensify the discomforts of the situation.

"I'm Kurnal Jarvis, zur. What kin I do for you?"

"I am adrift here, and cannot return for some hours. The mail man said perhaps Mrs. Jarvis would get me a cup of coffee."

The colonel smiled unctuously; replied, with a wave of his hand, that he did not keep a hotel, or in fact a house of entertainment of any kind, but that since the closing — he should say the collapse — of the Ocomoke Hotel he had prevailed upon Mrs. Jarvis to spread a humble table for the comfort and restoration of the wayfarer and stranger. If I would do him the honor of preceding him through the folding-doors to the right, he would conduct me to Mrs. Jarvis, a chop, and a cup of coffee.

I did him the honor at once, and was the next moment confronted by a little woman in a brown calico dress, who hung my wet coat on a clothes-horse by the fire with so many expressions of sympathy that my heart was won on the spot.

The breakfast was fairly good, although the vivid imagination of the colonel was not wholly realized, — Mrs. Jarvis substituting hot corn-bread and a sliver of bacon for the chop, and filling my cup with a weak decoction of toasted

173

sweet-potato skins and chicory in place of the divine essence of old Mocha.

Comforted by her gentle manner, and glad of any excuse to kill time until the 2.10 train should rescue me from what promised to be a most forlorn experience, I drew from her, little by little, not only her own history, but that of her unfortunate neighbors.

It seemed that some years back a capitalist from New York, uniting with other money-bags from Richmond, had fixed upon the town of Squantico as presenting, by reason of its location, extraordinary advantages for river and rail transportation; that, in pursuance of this scheme, they had bought up all the land in and around the village, had staked out numerous avenues and town lots, erected an imposing hotel surmounted by a cupola, and had started an immense pile dock trampling out into the river; that they had surveyed and partly graded a certain railroad, described as a " sixty-pound steel-rail and iron-bridge road," having one terminus on the wandering dock, and the other in a network of arteries connecting with the " heart of the whole Southern system ;" that, besides these local and contiguous improvements, such small trifles as a court - house of granite, a public

174

school of brick with stone trimmings, extensive water-works, and ridiculously cheap gas were to be immediately erected and introduced. All these enlargements, improvements, and benefits were duly set forth in a large circular, or hand-bill, with head-lines in red ink, a fly-specked copy being still visible tacked up behind the colonel's bar. In addition to these gratuities, large discounts were offered to the earliest settlers purchasing town lots and erecting structures thereon, the terms being within reach of the poorest, — one fourth cash, and the balance in three yearly installments of an equal amount.

Beguiled by these conditions and prospects, the colonel had sold her farm on the James River, — it was all she had in the world, an inheritance from her father's estate, — had moved their household effects to Squantico, paid the first installment, and erected the store and dwelling. This had absorbed their means.

All went well for the first year, or until the hotel was finished. Then came the collapse. One morning all work ceased on the dock and railroad. Another capitalist, of pointedly opposite views from the original group of projectors, had gobbled up the road-bed of the

175

projected railway, and had carried its terminus far out of reach of Squantico, and miles down the river. This had occurred some three years back.

Since that date a complicated melancholy had settled down over Squantico; the proprietors of the hotel had closed its doors from sheer famine, — not so much from want of something to eat as for want of somebody to eat it, — the unfinished dock had gone to decay, and the town to ruin. Squantico had shriveled up like a gourd in a September frost.

Nor was this all. Since the collapse no one had been able to meet the second payment on the land; the original capitalists wanted their pound of flesh; foreclosure proceedings had already been begun, and the act of dispossession was to be taken at the next spring term of the county court. Everybody in the village was in the same plight. "And indeed, sir," she added with a break in her voice, "what is to become of us! It will seem so hard to have no home at all."

I did what I could to divert her thoughts from her impending misfortunes by telling her something of my trip the night before, extracting for her benefit what little humor the situation afforded, and then, leaving her to the

176

care of her dishes, started out into the store.

The colonel widened the circle about the stove, turned to the three other chair holders, and introduced me as "My friend, Major"— and paused for my name. As I did not supply it, he glanced toward my bag for relief, caught sight of a baggage label pasted across one end, marked "B., Room —, N. Y.," and went straight on, as serene as an auctioneer with a fictitious bid.

"Broom, — Major Broom, — gentlemen, from New York."

The occupants stood erect for an instant, looked at me from under the rims of their hats, and sank into their chairs again.

If the title was a surprise to me, I being a plain landscape-painter, without capitals of any kind before or after my patronymic, the effrontery of displacing it by an express company's check simply took away my breath. But I did not correct him. It was not worth the while. He thanked me with his eye for my forbearance, and placed a chair at my disposal.

This eye of the colonel, by the way, was not the least interesting feature of his face. It was a moist, watery eye, suggestive of a system of accounts kept

mostly in chalk on a set of books covering half the swinging doors in the
county. From between these watery
spots protruded a sharp, beak-like nose.

My host connected these two features
by placing his forefinger longitudinally
along his nose until the nail closed the
right optic, and remarked, in a dry, husky
voice, that it was about his time, and
would I join him ? Instantly three pairs
of legs dropped from the stove rail, an
equal number of chairs were emptied,
and their occupants filed through a
green door with the paint worn off below the knob. I excused myself on the
ground of a late breakfast, and while
they were absent made an inspection of
the interior. It consisted of one long
room, on each side of which ran a pine
counter. This was littered up with
scraps of wrapping paper, a mouldy
cheese covered by a wire fly screen,
some cracker boxes, and a case with a
glass top containing small piles of plug
tobacco and some jars of stick candy.
Behind these counters were ranged pine
shelves, holding the usual assortment of
hardware, dry goods, canned vegetables,
and groceries. On the bottom shelf lay
a grillage of bar soap, left out to dry.
All the top shelves were packed with
empty boxes, — labels outside, — indicat-

178

ing to the unpracticed eye certain proba-
ble commercial resources.

Outside the rain fell in a drizzle, and
the fog settled in wavy wreaths.   Along
the road staggered a single team —
horse and mule tandem — harnessed, or
rather tied up, in clothes - lines, and
drawing a cart as large as a shoe box,
loaded with cord-wood, the whole followed by a negro clothed in cowhide
boots, an old army coat, and a straw
hat.   The movement was slow, but sure
enough to convince me that they had
not all died in their tracks overnight.

I followed this team with my eye
until the fog swallowed it up ; watched
a flock of geese pick their way across
the road, the leader's nose high in the
air, as if disgusted with the day ; went
over in my mind the delay of preparing
the breakfast, the time lost in its disposal, the long talk with Mrs. Jarvis,
and my many experiences since, and
concluded that it must be high noon.
I looked at my watch, and a chill crept
down my spine.   It was but a quarter
past nine !

Five hours more !

Disheartened but not wholly cast
down, I rummaged over a lot of wrapping paper, borrowed a pencil, and made
outline sketches of some pigeons drying

their feathers under the eaves of the stable roof; interviewed the boy feeding the pigs; listened enviously to their contented grunts; and at last, in sheer desperation, returned to the store and sat down. The hours were leaden. Would I never get away? Soon I began to have murderous intentions toward the porter. I remembered his exact expression when he promised the night before to wake me at eight o'clock. I could have sworn, on thinking it over, that he knew I was in the wrong car, and had concealed the fact, tempted by the opulence expressed in my new London bag. I felt that it had all been a devilish scheme to rob me of a double quarter, and throw me out into the mud in this thaw-stricken town.

In my broodings I began to take in the colonel, following his movements around the store, wondering whether he was not in the conspiracy, and had set the clock back to insure my missing the train.

A moment's reflection convinced me of the absurdity of all my misgivings, and I resolved to rise to the occasion. Mark Tapley could have made a gala-day of it. I would brace up and study the citizens.

The colonel was waiting on a customer,

—the only real one I had seen, —a mu-
latto girl with a jug.

"Misser Jarvis, Miss 'Manthy sez dat
thimble w'at you sent her las' week wuz
ur i'on thimble, an' she want ur steel
one. An' shè sez ef yer ain't got no
steel one she want ur squart o' molasses."

"Where 's the thimble?" said the
colonel.

" I drap it in de snow-bank out yer, —
'deed an' double I did, —an' I 'most froze
lookin' fur 't."

The colonel sighed.

While he was filling the jug, an old
man in an overcoat made from a gray
army blanket, and dragging by the muz-
zle a long Kentucky rifle, straggled in
and asked for a box of percussion caps
and half a pound of powder. Then resting his shooting-iron against the counter,
and pushing his long, skinny, cramped
hands through his coat - sleeves, he
opened out his thin fingers before the
stove and ventured the remark that it
was "right smart chilly."

"Any game, uncle?" I inquired.

"Mostly turkeys, zur ; but they's git-
tin' miz'ble sca'ce lately. 'Fo' de wah
't warn't nuthin' to git a passel of turkeys 'fore breakfas'. But you can't git
'em now. Dese yer scand'l'us-back
ducks is mo' plenty than they wuz ; but
181

ther ain't no gret shucks on 'em nary way."

The colonel handed the old man his ammunition, replaced a cracker box, threw his legs over the counter, and took the chair next me, his heels on the rail.

"Here on business, major?"

"No; pleasure," I replied wearily.

"Sorry the weather is so bad, zur; Squantico is not looking its best. Had you been here some few years ago, it would have looked dif'rent to you, zur."

"You mean before the scheme started?"

"Scheme or swindle, either way, zur. Perhaps you know Mr. Isaac Hoyle?"

I expressed my ignorance.

"Or have heard of the Squantico Land and Improvement Company?"

I was equally at fault, except what I had learned through Mrs. Jarvis.

"Then, zur, you are in no way connected with the gang of scoundrels who would rob us of our homes?"

I assured him that he had hit it exactly.

"Allow me to shake you by the han', zur, and offer you an apology. We took you for a lawyer, zur, from New York, come down about these fo'closure pro-

ceedin's. Will you join me?" All
the legs came down simultaneously with
a bang, but my firmness prevailed, and
they were slowly elevated once more.

"What are, you going to do about the
matter?" I asked.

"What can we do, zur? We are
bound hand and foot. We are prostrate,
zur, prostrate."

"Do?" said I, a ray of hope lighting
up my spirits. Perhaps, after all, there
were mitigating circumstances about
this enforced imprisonment. "Would
you have built this house if Hoyle had
not agreed to build his railroad?"

"Of co'se not," said the colonel.

"Did he build?"

"Not a foot."

"Did you?"

"Certainly."

"Well, then, colonel, sue Hoyle."

The colonel rose from his chair and
fixed upon me his drier eye. The loun-
gers straightened up and formed a circle.

"Are there any water-works, granite
school-houses, city halls, and other such
metropolitan luxuries around?" I continued.

The colonel shook his head.

"Had these been erected, and had the
programme as marked out in that be-
spattered circular behind your door been

carried out, would you be as poor as you are, or would you not now have a warehouse across the road to hold your surplus stock, and three wagons constantly backed up before your door to serve your customers? I tell you, sue Isaac Hoyle." .

"Kurnal," said Jarvis, — I did not correct the promotion, — "would you have any objection to elucidate yo' views befo' some of our leadin' citizens? They indicate a grasp of this subject, zur, which is giant-like, — yez, zur, giant-like! Jedge Drummond and Gen'ral Lownes are at this moment in the post-office, — two ve'y remarkable men, zur, quite our fo'most citizens. Might I send for 'em?"

"I would be delighted to meet the gentlemen." It might consume an hour. "Send for them, my dear sir; nothing would give me greater pleasure."

"Here, Joe," said the colonel, calling a negro who had lounged in from the road, and was now hovering on the outside of the circle; "g'w'up to the post-office, and tell Jedge Drummond and Gen'ral Lownes to come yer quick." The boy shuffled out, and Jarvis laid his hand on my shoulder. "It's a pleasure, kurnal, a gen-u-ine pleasure, zur, to meet a man of yo' calibre. Allow me to grasp

184

yo' han', and ask you before the arrival of my friends to "—

There was a slight movement toward the green door with the paint worn off, but I checked it before the sentence was complete.

"No! Well, zur, we will make it later. By the way, kurnal, before I forget it," —the colonel locked his arm through mine and led me aside, — "do not offer Mrs. Jarvis any compensation for yo' breakfast. She comes of a very high family, zur, and has a very sensitive nature. Of course, if you insist, I"—and my trade dollar dropped without a sound into his desolate pocket. "Here, boy! Did you fin' the gentlemen?"

"De gin'ral done gone duckin', sah, 'fore daylight, but the jedge say he is comin' right away scat."

The judge was on the boy's heels. As he entered, his eye wandered restlessly toward the paint-worn door. He had evidently misunderstood the message. I arose to greet him, the ring of listeners widening out to do justice to the impending ceremony. While the colonel squared himself for the opening address, I took in the general outline of the judge. He was the exact opposite of my host, — a short, fat, shad-shaped man of some fifty years or more, whose later life had

185

been spent in a ceaseless effort to keep his clothes up snug around the waist, his failures above being recorded in the wrinkles of his almost buttonless coat, and his successes below in the bagging of his trousers at the knee. He wore low shoes that did not match, and white cotton stockings a week old. A round, good-natured face, ornamented by a mustache dyed brown and a stump of a cigar, surmounted the whole.

"Jedge Drummond," began the colonel, "I sent my servant for you, zur, to introduce you to my ve'y particular friend, Gen'ral Broom, of the metropolis, zur, who is visiting the South, and who dropped in upon us this morning to breakfast. Gen'ral Broom, zur, is one of the most remark'ble men of the day, and, although a soldier like ourselves, has devoted himself since the wah to the practice of the law, and now stands at the zenith, the ve'y zenith, zur, of his p'ofession."

The judge expressed himself as overwhelmed, extended three fingers, and corrugated his vest pattern into wrinkles in the effort to squeeze himself between the arms of a chair. Jarvis then continued : —

."Gen'ral Broom is deeply interested in the misfortunes which have overtaken

186

Squantico, and has given expression to some ideas lookin' to'ards our vested rights which are startlin', zur. Gen'ral, will you kindly repeat yo' views to the jedge ?"

I did so briefly. To my mind it was simply a matter of contract. A grasping land company had staked out a comparative wilderness, and as an inducement to innocent investors and settlers had made certain promises, which, under the circumstances, were binding agreements. These agreements covered the erection of certain important municipal buildings, public conveniences, and improvements, together with a hotel, a dock, and a railroad. Only a fraction, a very small fraction, of these had been carried out. I would remind them, furthermore, that these agreements were distributed broadcast, and if not in writing, were in print, which in this case was the same thing. Relying on these documents, certain capitalists, like my friend Colonel Jarvis, had invested a very large portion of their surplus in erecting structures suitable only for a city of considerable commercial importance. The result was a matter of history. Squantico had yielded to a pressure greater than she could bear.

Judge Drummond closed both eyes as

if in deep thought, shifted his cigar, and remarked that the argument "was a sledge-hammer." He was delighted at the opportunity of knowing a man with so colossal a grasp.

The store began filling up, — the hurried exit of the boy and the instantaneous return of the judge having had its effect on the several citizens who had witnessed the occurrence. With each new arrival I was obliged to make a fresh statement, the colonel enlarging upon my abilities and rank until I began to shudder lest he should land me either in the White House, or upon the Supreme Bench.

I was beginning afresh on the last arrival — a weazen-faced old fellow with one tooth — when a fog-choked whistle sounded down the river, and every man except Jarvis and the judge filed out, crossed the road, and waited on the end of the unfinished dock until a wheezy side-wheel boat landed a negro woman and a yellow-painted trunk. This absorbing ceremony, paralyzing the industries of Squantico, I learned, occurred every day. As soon as the excitement calmed down and order had been restored, Jarvis executed a peculiar sign with his left eye; three citizens, including the judge, understood it, followed

him into a corner, consulted for a moment, and returned, the colonel leading.

"Major-Gen'ral Broom," said he, placing his hand on his heart, "yo' masterly
anal'sis of our rights in this fo'closure
matter convinces us that, if we are to
be protected at all, we must place ourselves in yo' han's. We know that yo'
duties are overwhelmin' and yo' time pre-
cious; but if you would consent to accept
a retainer, and appear for these cases at
the spring meeting of the county co'te
in April, we shall consider them settled.
What amount would you fix?"

The idea appalled me, but I was in
for it. "Gentlemen," I said, "your confidence, stranger as I am to most of you,
is embarrassing. As my main purpose
would be to wrest from this grasping
monopoly property which, if not yours,
should be, I would be willing to accept
only a small portion of the amount I
might recover as my fee" — at this
point Jarvis had great difficulty in re-
straining the outburst — "together — together, gentlemen, with a trifling cash
payment" — the noise moderated —
"which could be placed in the hands of
Colonel Jarvis, to be used for prelimi-
nary expenses."

A dead silence ensued. My selection
189

for stake-holder had evidently cast a chill over the room. This hardened into a frigid disapproval when the judge, voicing the assemblage, remarked that the "colonel would take good care of all the cash *he would get.*" Had not Mrs. Jarvis announced dinner, the situation would have become oppressive. The colonel punctured the stillness by instantly subscribing for his proportion, and asked the judge what amount he would contribute. That legal luminary rose slowly, picked up a crumb of cheese that had escaped the fly screen, and remarked that he would look over the list of his real estate and see. An audible smile permeated the crowd, the old sportsman's share widening into a grin, with an aside all to himself: "Real 'state? Golly! Reckon he kearries mos' of it on his shoes."

"My dear," said the colonel, as we followed his wife into the dining-room, "you of co'se understan' that to-day my old friend the gen'ral is our guest."

That gentle lady, who had borne the heat and burden of my entertainment alone, only replied with her eyes. I dropped another coin of the realm into the colonel's pocket to alleviate the loneliness of my contribution of the morning, lifted my hat to the sad little woman, who watched us wistfully through the half-opened door, her apron over her head, and took up my line of march to the station with just ten minutes to spare, the colonel carrying my bag, and about all the male population of Squantico serving as escort except the judge, who excused himself on the ground that he had "left his rubbers in his office." When I go South now, I pass Squantico in the night.